WORLD
WILDLIFE
QUIZ

DEEP NARAYAN PANDEY

THE RUPA BOOK OF
WORLD WILDLIFE QUIZ

THE RUPA BOOK OF
WORLD WILDLIFE QUIZ

DEEP NARAYAN PANDEY

RUPA

Published by
Rupa Publications India Pvt. Ltd 2004
7/16, Ansari Road, Daryaganj
New Delhi 110002

Sales centres:

Allahabad Bengaluru Chennai
Hyderabad Jaipur Kathmandu
Kolkata Mumbai

ISBN: 978-81-716-7079-6

Sixth impression 2017

10 9 8 7 6

FOR
THE .WILDERNESS-FRIENDLY PEOPLE
OF THE WORLD

ACKNOWLEDGEMENTS

I am grateful to my colleagues and officers in the Indian Forest Service who have helped me understand Tropical Forestry and Wildlife Management. Special thanks to: Samir Dubey, S.K. Verma, Rajesh Gopal, V.D. Sharma, Dr. S.N. Rai, S. Deb Roy, Dr. S.S. Negi, Dr. Ram Prasad, S.K. Pande, D.C. Sood, Abhijit Ghose, A.P. Dwivedi, D.P. Govil, R.N. Mehrotra, R.G. Soni, N. Uday Shekar, S.L. Wadhera, Sankatha Prasad, H.M. Bhatia, S.N. Bhise, C.S. Ratnasamy, Ashwini K. Upadhaya, G.V. Reddy, A.S. Brar, Dhananjai Mohan and Nitin Kakodkar.

I have benefited greatly from discussions with leading environmentalists, conservationists, and administrators, including Mrs. Maneka Gandhi, Samar Singh, H.S. Panwar, Dr. M.K. Ranjitsinh, Kailash Sankhala, Madhav Gadgil, J.C. Daniel, Bittu Sahgal, Anil Agarwal, Sunderlal Bahuguna, Chandi Prasad Bhatt, Dr. Ramchandra Guha, Shekhar Singh, W.A. Rodgers, Valmik Thapar, Fateh Singh Rathore, Jaswant Singh Nathawat, A.J.T. Johnsingh, Shantanu Kumar, S. Dillon Ripley and Sir Martin Ewans. I am indebted to them all.

I owe a special debt of gratitude to Professor S.C. Sinha, V.V. Kotia, K. Rajpal Singh, Jai Narayan Pandey, Gopal Pandey, Kailash Sankhala, A.S. Champawat, S.K. Pal, Johnson Thomas and Anil Computers, Udaipur, for the help they rendered me.

My parents permitted me to roam freely in the forests adjoining our village in pursuit of my 'wild' hobbies — watching birds and collecting wild plants. My wife, Pushpa, and children, Neha and Pushp Deep, are continuing the tradition where my parents left.

All of them are a great source of inspiration and encouragement.

DNP

CONTENTS

PREFACE

We require wild plants and animals for food and nutrition, clothing and construction, fuel and energy, medicine and ornamentation and above all, to enjoy the numerous life forms present in their myriad colours on Earth.

But our needs and dependence on Nature have resulted in the use, overuse and abuse of the species and ecosystem. Forests and woodlands are destroyed by over-exploitation for timber; grasslands are destroyed by conversion into farmlands and overgrazing by domestic livestock; wetlands are threatened by drainage for farming and construction. Environment is being polluted, thanks to industrialization and luxurious modern living. Our oceans and mangroves are threatened by exploitation beyond regenerative capacity. Man, through the corridors of time, has sent several species of plants and animals into oblivion. But is this resource rape sustainably enjoyable? No, many of us believe, absolutely not. And that is why we ought to know the diversity and fragility of life present in the major ecosystems of the world. Living resource conservation is necessary to maintain the essential ecological processes on which our survival and socio-economic development depend.

These factors operating, what should be done to save civilization on earth? Areas with exceptional biotic diversity may be declared as national parks and protected areas, and educational campaigns launched to make people aware of the need for conservation. We have to make informed choices for energy, economy and environment to produce more with limited resources.

With this in mind, I have presented the facts on the species and ecosystems of the world, and their conservation for sustainable development. *1000 World Wildlife Quiz* contains information on wildlifers, environmentalists, literature, biogeography, ecosystem, plants, forests, mammals, birds, reptiles, amphibians, fishes and insects, international co-operation, projects, conventions, legislation, organizations, sustainable development, national parks and protected areas of the world. It also deals with the behavioural studies and management of wildlife. In broader perspective, this book is an independent supplement to my earlier book entitled *Indian Wildlife Quiz*. Here and there, some facts may overlap, for a book on world wildlife cannot overlook mention of the richness of Indian wildlife, but in most instances I have provided new and interesting facts on a variety of plants, animals and ecosystems.

I hope the book will equip you to make informed choices in natural resource conservation and economic development.

DNP

1

GLIMPSES OF WORLD WILDLIFE

1. The unique Charity Bird Hospital was floated by Acharya Shanti Sagar of Digambar Jain Temple in 1926 as a first-aid centre. It became a charity hospital for birds in 1957. Where is it located?

   (a) Delhi (b) Madras (c) Patna (d) Satna

2. Name the only animal on earth, other than man, known to contract leprosy:

   (a) Ninebanded Armadillo (*Dasypus novem-cinctus*) (b) Elk (*Alces alces*) (c) Tiger (*Panthera tigris*) (d) King Cobra (*Ophiophagus hannah*)

3. Name the tiger specialists who provided the first ever photographic evidence of the role of the male tiger in post-natal care and peaceful interaction with its cubs, thus refuting charges against it of infanticide:

   (a) Kailash Sankhala and Guy Mountfort (b) Valmik Thapar and Fateh Singh Rathore (c) Jim Corbett and Keshri Singh (d) H.S. Panwar and Gustav Krik

4. Identify the person who wrote against the exhibition of trick-performing animals in a zoo: 'A zoo is not a circus and a zoo director has no business to be a ringmaster':

   (a) Kailash Sankhala (b) Peter Jackson (c) Charles McDougal (d) Theodore H. Reed

5. What management strategy is followed to keep populations of the African elephant in

balance with native vegetation of reserves where they have become over-abundant?

(a) Culling (b) Live-trapping and translocation (c) Habitat manipulation (d) Removal of competing species

6. Who wrote the autobiographical book, *My Life: My Trees?*

(a) Joy Adamson (b) Richard St. Barbe Baker (c) Konard Lorenz (d) K.M. Tewari

7. In which biogeographical realm does most part of the Asian continent fall?

(a) Nearctic realm (b) Neotropical realm (c) Palaearctic realm (d) Oriental realm

8. During the ice-sheeted pleistocene age some areas escaped from being covered by ice and acted as 'habitat islands' isolated from one another for long times and gave rise to several new species. What are these 'habitat islands' called?

(a) Pleistocene refugium (b) Ancient island (c) Green island (d) Islands of refuge

9. Name the endemic tree of Mauritius which stopped propagation, supposedly due to the extinction of the bird dodo (*Raphus cucullatus*), as seeds could germinate only when eaten and passed through the digestive tract of this bird:

(a) *Manilkara zapota* (b) *Calvaria major* (c) *Erythroxylon coca* (d) *Azadirachta indica*

10. Which tree yields the heaviest wood in the world?

(a) Black Iron Wood (*Olea laurifolia*) (b) Balsa (*Ochroma pyramidale*) (c) Durian (*Durio zibethinus*) (d) Mango (*Mangifera indica*)

11. Which is the only animal in the world to have four horns?

(a) Elk (*Alces alces*) (b) Chausingha (*Tetracerus quadricornis*) (c) Black Buck (*Antilope cervicapra*) (d) Bharal (*Pseudonis nayaur*)

12. Name the only country in the world where both the lion (*Panthera leo*) and the tiger (*Panthera tigris*) are found in the wild:

(a) Uganda (b) Zaire (c) Pakistan (d) India

13. A revolutionary but unpopular step is being taken in Namibia under the aegis of the *Operation Bicornis* to save the black rhino from eventual extinction from horn-poaching. What is the strategy?

(a) Tranquilizing and dehorning (b) Ranching all rhinos (c) Keeping all rhinos in zoos (d) Electrifying the fences of rhino reserves

14. Name the tanker that gutted itself on Bligh Reef and spilled 11 million gallons of crude oil into Alaska's Prince William Sound on March 24, 1989. The incident took the lives of more than 100,000 birds:

(a) *Sagar Kanya* (b) *Exxon Valdez* (c) *Amoco Cadiz* (d) *Hathi*

15. Which bird constructs the largest unit nest structure in the world?

(a) Red-billed Quelea (*Quelea quelea*) (b) Sociable Weaver (*Philetairus socius*) (c) Mountain Drongo (*Chaetorhynchus papuensis*) (d) Ostrich (*Struthio camelus*)

16. The Hawaiian goose (*Branta sandvicensis*) is an endemic bird of the Hawaiian Archipelago. Its number declined from an estimated 25,000 at the end of the century to less than 30 by

1952. About 1400 captive bred birds have been re-introduced in the wild to save the species from extinction. What is the popular name of this bird?

(a) Nene (b) Puaiohi (c) Kakapo (d) Tota

17. Name a snake found in South America that looks identical to the green python (*Chondropython viridis*) of New Guinea and Australia:

   (a) King Cobra (*Ophiophagus hannah*)
   (b) Reticulated Python (*Python reticulatus*)
   (c) Emerald Tree Boa (*Corallus caninus*)
   (d) Black Mamba (*Dendroapsis polylepsis*)

18. Which is the longest reptile in the world?.

   (a) King Cobra (*Ophiophagus hannah*)
   (b) Reticulated Python (*Python reticulatus*)
   (c) Emerald Tree Boa (*Corallus caninus*)
   (d) Black Mamba (*Dendroapsis polylepsis*)

19. Out of 150 species of frog in Madagascar, how many are endemic, i.e., found nowhere else in the world?

   (a) 100 (b) 128 (c) 140 (d) 148

20. Which terrestrial animal has the longest gestation period in the world?

   (a) Alpine Salamander (*Salamandra atra*)
   (b) Indian Elephant (*Elephas maximus*)
   (c) African Elephant (*Loxodonta africana*)
   (d) Tiger (*Panthera tigris*)

21. Which group of fish can remain out of water for the longest duration?

   (a) Salmon (b) Mudskipper (c) Hilsa
   (d) Shark

22. Which fish was used as an indicator of the levels of cadmium, mercury and zinc in the polluted waters of Germany?

(a) Golden Dragon (*Scleropagas formosus*) (b) Gold Fish (*Carassius auratus*) (c) Mosquito Fish (*Gambusia affinis*) (d) Rabbit Fish (*Siganus oramini*)

23. Which is the largest butterfly in the world?

(a) Birdwing Butterfly (*Ornithopteria allottei*) (b) Swallow-tail (*Papilio machan*) (c) Alexandra Birdwing (*Ornithopteria alexandrae*) (d) Monarch Butterfly (*Danaus plexippus*)

24. Though the monarch butterfly (*Danaus plexippus*) is found in millions, it is nevertheless endangered. Why?

(a) Roosting sites in North America face threat from logging, tourism, grazing and forest fires (b) Over-collection for souvenir (c) Over-predation by introduced predators (d) Non-breeding

25. Which is the world's largest private international nature conservation organization?

(a) Bombay Natural History Society (b) World Wide Fund for Nature (c) Audubon Society (d) Ranthambhore Foundation

26. Where is the headquarters of the International Council for Bird Preservation (ICBP) located?

(a) Cambridge (b) Jakarta (c) New Delhi (d) Bombay

27. The 'Convention of Wetlands of International Importance Especially as Waterfowl Habitat' was signed on February 2, 1971, in an Iranian

town and came into force on December 21, 1985. By what name is the convention popularly known?

(a) Bonn Convention (b) Ramsor Convention (c) Whaling Convention (d) Migratory Species Convention

28. Which document declares: 'Living resources shall not be utilized in excess of their natural capacity for regeneration'?

(a) World Conservation Strategy (b) World Charter for Nature (c) Bali Action Plan (d) Corbett Action Plan

29. The trans-frontier reserves of two or more countries provide a larger and better Protected Area Unit. Name the countries involved in the Ruwenzori-Virunga-volcanoes system of parks:

(a) Ethiopia, Kenya and Somalia (b) Zaire, Kenya and Somalia (c) Uganda, Zaire and Egypt (d) Uganda, Rwanda and Zaire

30. If we want to involve the native tribal population in the management of protected areas for sustainable use of natural resources and eco-development, what would be the best model to follow?

(a) National Park (b) Biosphere Reserve (c) World Heritage Site (d) Wildlife Sanctuary

WILLIFERS AND CONSERVATIONISTS

31. Who rediscovered the noisy scrub-bird (*Atrichornis clamosus*) of Australia in the year 1961 after its long believed extinction from 1889?

    (a) Harley Webster (b) Magellan (c) Bharat Bhusan (d) Kailash Sankhala

32. Name the explorer by whom the birds of paradise (*Paradisaeidae*) were made known to Europe:

    (a) Harley Webster (b) Magellan (c) Bharat Bhusan (d) Kailash Sankhala

33. Name the person who rediscovered the Jerdon's or Doublebanded Courser (*Cursorius bitorquatus*) in India:

    (a) Harley Webster (b) Magellan (c) Bharat Bhusan (d) Kailash Sankhala

34. Which Indian emperor formulated laws for wildlife preservation?

    (a) Babur (b) Akbar (c) Ashoka (d) Jafar

35. Name the person who is a tiger specialist and received the Jawaharlal Nehru Fellowship to undertake ecological and behavioural study of the Indian tiger (*Panthera tigris tigris*) in 1969:

    (a) Guy Mountfort (b) Kailash Sankhala (c) Indira Gandhi (d) Charles McMathias

36. Who said: 'Our ancestors had learned to live with them (wildlife) in mutual respect. We

had this great heritage in trust for future generations'?

(a) Guy Mountfort (b) Kailash Sankhala (c) Indira Gandhi (d) Charles McMathias

37. Who wrote: 'A tiger is a large-hearted gentleman with boundless courage and that when he is exterminated — as exterminated he will be unless public opinion rallies to his support — India will be poorer by having lost the finest of her fauna'?

(a) C. Dunkan (b) Indira Gandhi (c) Kailash Sankhala (d) Jim Corbett

38. Who was the vice-chairman of IUCN's Commission on National Parks and Protected Areas for Indo-Malayan Realm during the World Congress on National Parks and Protected Areas at Bali in 1982?

(a) Samar Singh (b) David Attenborough (c) Mark Dourojeanni (d) Martin Booth

39. Which naturalist is associated with a successful TV Series *Life On Earth* and *The Living Planet*?

(a) Samar Singh (b) David Attenborough (c) Mark Dourojeanni (d) Martin Booth

40. Name the person known as the 'Man of the Trees':

(a) Katharine Payne (b) William Langbauer (c) Richard St. Barbe Baker (d) Jane Goodal

41. Who was the vice-chairman of IUCN's Commission on National Parks and Protected Areas for Afrotropical Realm during the World Congress on National Parks and Protected Areas held at Bali in 1982?

(a) Walter Lusigi (b) Birendra Singh (c) J. Westoby (d) Martin Ewans

42. Which Indian woman is known as the 'Snake Lady'?

   (a) Zai Whitaker (b) Manjoo Singh (c) Royina Grewal (d) Joanna Van Gruisen

43. Name the person associated with the famous tree protection movement 'Chipko' in India:

   (a) Sunderlal Bahuguna (b) Chandi Prasad Bhatt (c) Both the above (d) S. Deb Roy

44. Which Indian forester was recently awarded the Queen's Award for Forestry (Commonwealth Forestry Award)?

   (a) J.C. Daniel (b) A.R. Rahmani (c) S. Deb Roy (d) S.N. Rai

45. Which Indian forester was awarded the N. Borlog Award in the year 1987 for his meritorious efforts in the conservation of wild genetic resources in India?

   (a) S. Deb Roy (b) S.N. Rai (c) A.P. Dwivedi (d) J.C. Daniel

46. Writing about the grand success of the world's largest and most successful conservation project, *Project Tiger*, in India, who wrote: 'The Project has fully demonstrated that by tradition and training the Indian forester is much better equipped to administer a conservation project than anyone else; this view is shared by my friends the American foresters who manage wildlife habitats'?

   (a) Kailash Sankhala (b) Fateh Singh Rathore (c) H.S. Panwar (d) Guy Mountfort

47. Name the person about whom Jan Morris wrote: 'To say that he is a tiger addict would be a preposterous understatement. He is an *honorary tiger* himself....':

(a) Kailash Sankhala (b) S. Deb Roy (c) Jim Corbett (d) Martin Booth

48. Name the person who represented India and was chairman of Convention on International Trade in Endangered Species of Wild Flora and Fauna (CITES) for three successive terms from 1981 to 1985?

    (a) Samar Singh (b) J.B. Lal (c) H.S. Panwar (d) P. Singh

49. In which field of conservation is Sally Walker considered an authority?

    (a) National Park Management (b) Zoo Management (c) Forest Management (d) Wildlife Management

50. Name the conservationist who made the films *Treasures of Corsica, Animal Paradise, Grand Safari*, and *Let Them Live* based on worldwide explorations:

    (a) Christian Zuber (b) Sally Walker (c) Sir Peter Scott (d) Rajpal Singh

51. Name the person whose painting titled *Tiger Fire* and its prints helped to raise £ 1,12,000 for the movement to save the tiger from extinction:

    (a) Christian Zuber (b) David Shepherd (c) Gerald Cubitt (d) Rajpal Singh

52. Name the world's leading freelance natural history photographer who toured the Indian subcontinent and produced, with a text by Guy Mountfort, one of the best photographic books on the Indian wilderness, *Wild India*, published by Collins in 1985:

    (a) Gerald Cubitt (b) Toby Sinclair (c) Naresh Bedi (d) Rajesh Bedi

53. Name the animal being studied by Dr. Jane Goodall for the last three decades at Gombe National Park, Tanzania:

    (a) Chimpanzee *(Pan troglodytes)* (b) Gorilla *(Gorilla gorilla)* (c) Orangutan *(Pongo pygmaeus)* (d) Lion *(Panthera leo)*

54. Name the animal being studied by Dr. Itani and Dr. Nishida at Mahale Mountain National Park, Tanzania:

    (a) Chimpanzee *(Pan troglodytes)* (b) Gorilla *(Gorilla gorilla)* (c) Orangutan *(Pongo pygmaeus)* (d) Lion *(Panthera leo)*

55. Who was the first president of the World Wildlife Fund (now World Wide Fund for Nature)?

    (a) Prince Bernhard of the Netherlands (b) Sir Peter Scott (c) Sir David Attenborough (d) Sir Martin Ewans

56. In which year did the late J. Paul Getty institute the award of the same name which is popularly called 'Nobel Prize of Conservation'?

    (a) 1970 (b) 1974 (c) 1976 (d) 1986

57. Who was the founder chairman of WWF (World Wild Fund for Nature)?

    (a) Jane Goodall (b) Sir Peter Scott (c) Salim Ali (d) Ian Prestt

58. What is the subject of the study of Jane Goodall?

    (a) Primatology (b) Ornithology (c) Herpetology (d) Geology

59. Who is the founder of the science of animal behaviour — Ethology?

(a) Richard St. Barbe Baker (b) Konard Lorenz (c) Jane Goodall (d) P. Andrew

60. Over-grazing in protected areas by domestic livestock leads to dominance of unpalatable species, reduction in palatable trees, invasion of weeds, reduction in total biomass and nutrient pool, increased rates of run-off and evaporation from surface soil. Repeated localized over-grazing results in soil erosion and soil compaction due to treading. In the year 1987 *Operation Green Carpet* was launched to save Ranthambhore Tiger Reserve from illicit grazing by domestic livestock. The Operation was a brainchild of the then director of Ranthambhore Tiger Reserve. He mobilised the staff, vehicles, wireless network and other resources of the *Project Tiger* including support from police. Name him:
(a) Jaswant Singh Nathawat (b) Samir Dubey
(c) Fateh Singh Rathore (d) Kailash Sankhala

3
LITERATURE ON WILDERNESS

61. Who wrote the book *The Worst Journey in the World?*
(a) Apsley Cherry Garrard (b) David Lack
(c) Oliver Austin (d) David Attenborough

62. Who is the author of the book *Wild America* published by Collins in 1956?
(a) R.T. Peterson and J. Fisher (b) E. Howard
(c) D. Lack (d) David Attenborough

63. Who wrote the book *Territory in Bird Life* published by Collins in 1964?
    (a) R.T. Peterson and J. Fisher (b) E. Howard (c) D. Lack (d) David Attenborough

64. Who is the author of *The Life of the Robin* published by Witherby in 1943?
    (a) R.T. Peterson and J. Fisher (b) E. Howard (c) D. Lack (d) David Attenborough

65. Who wrote the book *Eagles, Hawks and Falcons of the World* published by Country Life in 1968?
    (a) J. Delacour (b) J.M. Forshaw (c) L. Brown and D. Amadon (d) D. Lack

66. Who wrote the book *Parrots of the World* published by Lansdowne in 1973?
    (a) J. Delacour (b) J.M. Forshaw (c) L. Brown and D. Amadon (d) D. Lack

67. Who wrote the book *The Waterfall of the World* in four volumes, published by Country Life between 1954 and 1964?
    (a) J. Delacour (b) J.M. Forshaw (c) L. Brown and D. Amadon (d) Salim Ali

68. Who wrote the book *Birds of the World* published by Hamlyn in 1962?
    (a) Oliver L. Austin (b) S.V. Benson (c) G.M. Henry (d) Salim Ali

69. Who wrote the book *Birds of Ceylon* published by Oxford University Press in 1955?
    (a) Oliver L. Austin (b) S.V. Benson (c) G.M. Henry (d) Salim Ali

70. Who wrote the book *Birds of Lebanon* published by ICBP in 1970?

(a) Oliver L. Austin (b) S.V. Benson (c) G.M. Henry (d) Salim Ali

71. Who is the author of *The Palearctic — African Bird Migration Systems* published by Academic Press in 1972?

    (a) K.H. Voous (b) B.E. Smythies (c) R.E. Moreau (d) Salim Ali

72. Who is the author of the *Atlas of European Birds* published by Nelson in 1960?

    (a) K.H. Voous (b) B.E. Smythies (c) R.E. Moreau (d) Salim Ali

73. Who is the author of *The Birds of Burma* published by Oliver and Boyd in 1953?

    (a) K.H. Voous (b) B.E. Smythies (c) R.E. Moreau (d) Salim Ali

74. Who wrote the *Handbook of North American Birds* published by Yale in 1962?

    (a) R.S. Palmer (b) J. Bond (c) F. Haverschmidt (d) David Lack

75. Who wrote the book *Birds of the West Indies* published by Collins in 1960?

    (a) R.S. Palmer (b) J. Bond (c) F. Haverschmidt (d) David Lack

76. Who wrote the book *Birds of Surinam* published by Oliver and Boyd in 1968?

    (a) R.S. Palmer (b) J. Bond (c) F. Haverschmidt (d) David Lack

77. Who wrote *The Birds of the Republic of Panama* published by Smithsonian Institution in 1968?

    (a) A. Wetmore (b) D.A. Bannerman (c) R.D. Etchecopar and F. Hue (d) B. Marston

78. Who wrote *The Birds of North Africa* published by Oliver and Boyd in 1967?

(a) A. Wetmore (b) D.A. Bannerman (c) R.D. Etchecopar and F. Hue (d) J. Bond

79. Who wrote the book *Birds of West and Equatorial Africa* in two volumes published by Oliver and Boyd during 1951 to 1953?

    (a) A. Wetmore (b) D.A. Bannerman (c) R.D. Etchecopar and F. Hue (d) E. Mayr

80. Who wrote the *African Handbook of Birds* published by Longman in six volumes between 1952 and 1973?

    (a) A. Rand (b) Martin Ewans (c) E. Mayr (d) C.W. Mackworth Praed and C.H.B. Grant

81. Who is the author of *The Forest and the Sea* published by Random House in 1965?

    (a) B. Marston (b) Rachel Carson (c) J.W. Coll and E.R. Wolf (d) Martin Ewans

82. Who wrote the book *The Edge of the Sea* published by Houghton Miffin in 1955?

    (a) B. Marston (b) Rachel Carson (c) J.W. Coll and E.R. Wolf (d) P. Odum

83. Who is the author of *The Hidden Frontier: Ecology and Ethnicity in an Alpine Valley* published by Head Press in 1974?

    (a) B. Marston (b) Rachel Carson (c) J.W. Coll and E.R. Wolf (d) J. Dorst

84. Who is the author of the book *Environment Power and Society* published by John Wiley & Sons in 1971?

    (a) H.T. Odum (b) F.M. Burnet (c) R.F. Dasmann (d) J. Dorst

85. Who is the author of *The Natural History of Infectious Diseases* published by Cambridge University Press in 1962?

(a) H.T. Odum (b) F.M. Burnet (c) R.F. Dasmann (d) R. Carson

86. Who is the author of the book *Ecological Principles for Economic Development* published by Wiley in 1973?
(a) H.T. Odum (b) F.M. Burnet (c) R.F. Dasmann (d) Arjan Singh

87. Who is the author of the book *Before Nature Dies* published by Houghton Miffin in 1970?
(a) J. Dorst (b) K. Hewit (c) C. Pomerantz (d) Ian Prestt

88. Who wrote *Lifeboat: Man and a Habitable Earth*?
(a) J. Dorst (b) K. Hewit (c) C. Pomerantz (d) Romulus Whitaker

89. Who wrote *The Day They Parachuted Cats on Bormo: A Drama of Ecology* in 1971?
(a) J. Dorst (b) K. Hewit (c) C. Pomerantz (d) R. Hill

90. Who wrote the book *Man in the Web of Life* published by New American Library in 1968?
(a) R. Lews (b) J.H. Storer (c) Martin Booth (d) P.K. Anderson

91. Who edited the book *National Parks, Conservation and Development: The Role of Protected Area in Sustaining Society* published in 1984 by IUCN and Smithsonian Institution?
(a) J.A. McNeely and K.R. Miller (b) T. Corfield (c) P.A. Jewell, S. Holt and D. Hart (d) Ian Prestt

92. Who wrote the book *The Wilderness Guardian* published by David Sheldrick Foundation in 1985?

(a) J.A. McNeely and K.R. Miller (b) T. Corfield (c) P.A. Jewell, S. Holt and D. Hart (d) Ian Prestt

93. Who edited the book *Problems in Management of Locally Abundant Wild Mammals* published by Academic Press in 1981?

(a) J.A. McNeely and K.R. Miller (b) T. Corfield (c) P.A. Jewell, S. Holt and D. Hart (d) Ian Prestt

94. Who wrote the book *Public Relations and Communications for Natural Resource Managers* published by Kendall/Hunt Publishing Co. in 1981?

(a) J.R. Fazio and D.L. Gilbert (b) S. Lyster (c) J.A. McNeely and D. Pitt (d) Anthony W. Diamond

95. Who is the author of *International Wildlife Law* published by Grotius in 1985?

(a) J.R. Fazio and D.L. Gilbert (b) S. Lyster (c) J.A. McNeely and D. Pitt (d) Anthony W. Diamond

96. Who edited the book *Culture* and *Conservation*: *The Human Dimension in Environment Planning* published by Croom Helm in 1985?

(a) J.R. Fazio and D.L. Gilbert (b) S. Lyster (c) J.A. McNeely and D. Pitt (d) Anthony W. Diamond

97. Who wrote the book *Planning National Parks for Eco-Development* published by the University of Michigan in 1978?

(a) K.R. Miller (b) Norman Myers (c) D. Poore (d) Ian Prestt

98. Who wrote the book *The Sinking Ark* in 1979 published by Pergamon?

(a) K.R. Miller (b) Norman Myers (c) D. Poore (d) Ian Prestt

99. Who wrote *Ecological Guidelines for Development in Tropical Rainforests* published by IUCN in 1976?

(a) K.R. Miller (b) Norman Myers (c) D. Poore (d) Ian Prestt

100. Who wrote the book *The Study and Management of Large Mammals* in 1982 published by John Wiley & Sons?

(a) T. Riney (b) R.V. Salm and J.R. Clark (c) D. Poore (d) Rudolf L. Wchreiber

101. Who wrote the book *Marine and Coastal Protected Areas: A Guide for Planners and Managers* published by IUCN in 1984?

(a) T. Riney (b) R.V. Salm and J.R. Clark (c) D. Poore (d) Rudolf L. Wchreiber

102. Which organization prepared a book *Teaching Conservation in Developing Nations* in 1977?

(a) World Wide Fund for Nature (b) Bombay Natural History Society (c) U.S. Peace Corps (d) World Bird Club

103. Which organization prepared a booklet *Categories, Objectives and Criteria for Protected Areas* in 1978?

(a) IUCN (b) WWF (c) UNEP (d) UNDP

104. Who compiled the book *Managing Protected Areas in The Tropics* published by IUCN/UNEP in 1986 based on the Workshop on Managing Protected Areas in the Tropics World Congress on National Parks at Bali in 1982?

(a) John and Kathy MacKinnon, Graham Child and Jim Thorsell (b) Samar Singh (c) Walter Lusigi (d) Ian Prestt

105. Who is the author of the book *Conserving India's Natural Heritage* published in 1986 by Natraj?
(a) Samar Singh (b) Dr. Salim Ali (c) Romulus Whitaker (d) Kailash Sankhala

106. Whose autobiography is *The Snake Man?*
(a) Samar Singh (b) Dr. Salim Ali (c) Romulus Whitaker (d) Kailash Sankhala

107. Who wrote the book *Tiger — Portrait of a Predator* published by Collins in 1986?
(a) Valmik Thapar, Gunter Ziesler and Fateh Singh Rathore (b) Kailash Sankhala (c) Arjan Singh (d) Samar Singh

108. Who illustrated the book *A Pictorial Guide to the Birds of the Indian Subcontinent* published by BNHS and Oxford University Press in 1983?
(a) John Henry Dick (b) S. Dillon Ripley (c) Fateh Singh Rathore and Tejbir Singh

109. Who is the author of the book *Search for Spiny Babbler?*
(a) John Henry Dick (b) S. Dillon Ripley (c) Fateh Singh Rathore and Tejbir Singh

110. Who wrote the remarkable book *Tiger* which was published by Collins in 1978?
(a) Kailash Sankhala (b) Arjan Singh (c) G.B. Schaller (d) M.L. Roonwal

111. Who said about the book *Tiger* that 'This book might be called the autobiography of a tiger addict'?

(a) Kailash Sankhala (b) Arjan Singh (c) G.B. Schaller (d) M.L. Roonwal

112. Who wrote the book *The Deer and the Tiger?*

(a) Kailash Sankhala (b) Arjan Singh (c) G.B. Schaller (d) M.L. Roonwal

113. Who wrote the book *Carpet Sahib — A Life of Jim Corbett* published by Oxford University Press?

(a) Martin Booth (b) J.C. Daniel (c) George Adamson (d) Bernhard Grizmek

114. Who is the author of the famous work *The Book of Indian Reptiles* published by BNHS and Oxford University Press?

(a) Martin Booth (b) J.C. Daniel (c) George Adamson (d) Bernhard Grizmek

115. Who wrote the book *My Pride and Joy?*

(a) Martin Booth (b) J.C. Daniel (c) George Adamson (d) Bernhard Grizmek

116. Who wrote the book *Jungle Life of India* published by Lustre Press in 1990?

(a) Nirmal Ghosh and Rajpal Singh (b) H.S. Panwar (c) Kailash Sankhala (d) Naresh Bedi

117. Name the wildlife and conservation magazine for children from the publishers of *Sanctuary Asia* magazine:

(a) *Pup* (b) *Nature* (c) *Wildlife* (d) *Cub*

118. Who wrote the well illustrated book *Indian Wildlife* in 1984?

(a) Naresh and Ramesh Bedi (b) Billy Arjan Singh (c) Dr. Salim Ali (d) Rajesh and Ramesh Bedi

119. Which book of Dr. Salim Ali is co-authored by S. Dillon Ripley?

(a) *Birds of Kutch* (b) *Birds of Sikkim* (c) *The Handbook of the Birds of India & Pakistan*

120. **Billy Arjan Singh** wrote four books as a result of studies in the forests of Uttar Pradesh and Dudhwa National Park in India. Three of these are *Tiger Haven, Tara — A Tigress* and *Tiger Tiger*. Which is the fourth book?

(a) *The Cats* (b) *The Snakeman* (c) *Tree Tops* (d) *The Prince of Cats*

121. Who wrote the book *Bharatpur: Bird Paradise* published by Lusture Press in 1989?

(a) Martin Ewans, Thakur Daleep Singh, K Rajpal Singh and J. Hancock (b) Salim Ali (c) H.S. Panwar (d) S. Dillon Ripley

122. Who wrote the book *Birds at Risk* published by Moonraker Press in 1981?

(a) R. Whitelock (b) M. Carwardine (c) Ian Prestt (d) Anthony W. Diamond

123. Who wrote the book *The Encyclopaedia of World Wildlife* published by Chartwell Books in 1986?

(a) R. Whitelock (b) M. Carwardine (c) Ian Prestt (d) Anthony W. Diamond

124. What information does the *Red Data Book* provide?

(a) Threatened and rare species of plants and animals (b) Taxa out of danger (c) Taxa permitted for trade (d) Taxa housed in national parks

125. What is the title of the book containing names of the rare plants growing in botanical gardens and protected areas?

(a) *Red Data Book* (b) *Green Book* (c) *Yellow Data Book* (d) *White Book*

126. Who wrote the book *With Tigers in the Wild?*
(a) Kailash Sankhala (b) Fateh Singh Rathore, Tejbir Singh and Valmik Thapar (c) H.S. Panwar (d) William G. Conway

127. Who wrote the book *Animals in Danger* published by Barrons, New York, in the year 1978?
(a) Christian Zuber (b) J.F. Bernard (c) Sir Peter Scott (d) Gustav Krik

128. The first zoo management book to be published in the world was *A Handbook of the Management of Animals in Captivity in Lower Bengal* that came out in the year 1892. Who wrote it?
(a) Sally Walker (b) Ram Brahma Sanyal (c) Salim Ali (d) Theodore H. Reed

129. Who wrote the books *Portrait of a Wilderness, Portrait of a Desert, The Vanishing Jungles, So Small a World* and *Saving the Tiger?*
(a) Kailash Sankhala (b) Guy Mountfort (c) Valmik Thapar (d) P. Andrew

130. Who wrote the book *Rare Birds of the World, A Collins and ICBP Handguide*, published by Collins in 1988?
(a) Guy Mountfort and Norman Arlott (b) David Attenborough (c) Martin Ewans (d) P. Andrew

131. Who wrote the book *Birds to Watch: The ICBP World Checklist of Threatened Birds* published by Cambridge and ICBP in the year 1988?

(a) N.J. Collar and P. Andrew (b) Guy Mountfort (c) David Attenborough (d) Gro Harlem Brundtland

132. Who wrote the book *Back from the Brink* published by Hutchinson in 1978?

(a) N.J. Collar and P. Andrew (b) Guy Mountfort (c) David Attenborough (d) Gro Harlem Brundtland

133. Who wrote the book *The Trials of Life* published by Collins and BBC in the year 1990?

(a) N.J. Collar and P. Andrew (b) Guy Mountfort (c) David Attenborough (d) Gro Harlem Brundtland

134. Who is the author of the famous trilogy *Life on Earth, The Living Planet* and *The Trials of Life?*

(a) N.J. Collar and P. Andrew (b) Guy Mountfort (c) David Attenborough (d) Gro Harlem Brundtland

135. Who wrote the book *Tigers — The Secret Life* published by Elm Tree Books in the year 1989?

(a) Valmik Thapar and Fateh Singh Rathore
(b) Kailash Sankhala (c) Guy Mountfort
(d) Malcolm Coe

136. Which journal is devoted to the study of Afrotropical ornithology?

(a) *Nature* (b) *Pavo* (c) *Tauraco* (d) *Birds*

137. Which journal is devoted to Indian ornithology?

(a) *Nature* (b) *Pavo* (c) *Tauraco* (d) *Birds*

138. Name an Asian ecology and wildlife bi-month-ly currently edited by environmentalist Bittu Sahgal:

(a) *Sanctuary Asia* (b) *Cub* (c) *Oryx* (d) *Pavo*

139. What is the new name of the Species Survival Commission Newsletter of the IUCN?

(a) *Species* (b) *Parks* (c) *Oryx* (d) *Pavo*

140. Who publishes the *Endangered Species Technical Bulletin?*

(a) US Fish and Wildlife Service (b) Indian Forest Service (c) Pakistan Forest Service (d) Nepal Forest Service

141. Name a news bulletin published by FAO Regional Office for Asia and the Pacific region dedicated to the exchange of infor-mation relating to Wildlife and National Parks Management for the Asia-Pacific Region:

(a) *Audubon* (b) *Ambio* (c) *Tigerpaper* (d) *Parks*

142. Which of the following journals are dedicated to the study of birds?

(a) *Ardea* (b) *Auk* (c) *Condor* (d) *Pavo*

143. Who wrote the book *Garden of Gods — Bird Sanctuary Bharatpur* published by Vikas Publishing House in 1990?

(a) K. Rajpal Singh (b) Kailash Sankhala (c) Sir Martin Ewans (d) Martin Booth

144. The first *Red Data Book* was published on mammals in the year 1966. Who compiled it?

(a) Noel Simon (b) Jack Vincent (c) Rene Honegger (d) Jack Westoby

145. The *Red Data Book* on birds was published immediately after the *Red Data Book: Mammals* in the year 1966. Who compiled it?

(a) Noel Simon (b) Jack Vincent (c) Rene Honegger (d) Jack Westoby

146. The *Red Data Book* on reptiles and amphibians was published in the year 1968. Who compiled it?

(a) Noel Simon (b) Jack Vincent (c) Rene Honegger (d) Jack Westoby

4

BIOGEOGRAPHY AND ECOSYSTEMS

147. In what kind of habitat have several species of frogs, snakes, lizards and mammals developed the gliding adaptation to move through the forest canopy?

(a) Tropical rain forests (b) Deciduous forests (c) Scrub forests (d) Moist forests

148. In what kind of forest have many species of monkeys, anteaters and pangolins developed prehensile tail as an adaptation for arboreal life?

(a) Tropical rain forests (b) Deciduous forests (c) Scrub forests (d) Moist forests

149. What is the distribution of the rain forests in the world?

(a) Discontinuous strip from South and South-East Asia (b) Asia (c) North America (d) Sri Lanka

150. What is the main cause for the destruction of the tropical rain forests?

(a) Shifting cultivation (b) Providing more land for agriculture (c) Commercial logging

151. In what kind of ecosystem is the colourful climber plant passion flower (*Passiflora vitifolia*) found?

(a) Rain forests (b) Deciduous forests (c) Alpine forests (d) Deserts

152. What is the distribution of temperate forests in the world?

(a) Central and Western Europe (b) Eastern USA, China and Japan (c) None of the above (d) Both the above

153. In which hemisphere are maximum temperate forests found?

(a) Southern (b) Northern (c) Not well defined

154. Once Britain had 70 per cent of its land area under temperate forest cover. What is the proportion today?

(a) 2% (b) 5% (c) 8% (d) 10%

155. In what kind of forests you find the oak, beach, maple and birch trees?

(a) Tropical rain forests (b) Temperate forests (c) Tropical cloudforests (d) Tropical swampforests

156. What area of the earth is covered with the tropical forests?

(a) 900 million ha. (b) 1,935 million ha. (c) 1,200 million ha. (d) 735 million ha.

157. Where are coniferous forests distributed more prominently?

(a) High latitudes and high altitudes (b) Low altitudes (c) High longitude (d) Low longitude

158. In what kind of forests you find the pine, fir, larch, spruce, redwood and hemlock?

(a) Rain forests (b) Temperate forests (c) Coniferous forests (d) Deciduous forests

159. What kind of forests are predominantly found in Siberia?

(a) Rain forests (b) Temperate forests (c) Coniferous forests (d) Deciduous forests

160. By what name are the coniferous forests known in North America and Europe?

(a) Taiga (b) Boreal forests (c) Pampa (d) Tundra

161. By what name are the coniferous forests known in major parts of Asia?

(a) Taiga (b) Boreal forests (c) Pampa (d) Tundra

162. What kind of forests are found at the southern edge of the boreal and taiga forests?

(a) Rain forests (b) Deciduous forests (c) Coniferous forests (d) Moist forests

163. In what kind of forest is moose (*Alces alces*) found?

(a) Coniferous forests (b) Rain forests (c) Tundra (d) Taiga

164. The area of which type of habitat is increasing in the world?

(a) Rain forests (b) Wetlands (c) Deserts (d) Kalahari

165. Which is the largest desert in the world?

(a) Thar (b) Sahara (c) Gobi (d) Kalahari

166. What is the evidence to show that part of the Sahara desert was once covered with vegetation and occupied by animals?

(a) Cave paintings (b) Fossils (c) Root stock (d) Woods and bones

167. What is the reason for desertification?

(a) Deforestation (b) Over-grazing and over-cropping (c) Wild fires (d) All the above

168. What is the percentage of landmass threatened with desertification affecting more than 100 countries?

(a) 30 (b) 50 (c) 75 (d) 95

169. Name the habitat found in two narrow strips, one along the Tropic of Cancer and the other along the Tropic of Capricorn, in the world:

(a) Rain forests (b) Coniferous forests (c) Deserts (d) Dry thorn forests

170. What is the distribution of tundra in the world?

(a) Northern edges of Europe, Asia and North America (b) Along the Tropics of Cancer and Capricorn (c) Southern edges of South America, Africa and Australia (d) All the above

171. What do you mean by the word "Tundra"?

(a) Desert (b) Full of trees (c) Treeless (d) Full of water

172. What is the latitudinal distribution of tundra in the world?

(a) Between 5 and 10 degrees north (b) Between 20 and 40 degrees north (c) Between 60 and 70 degrees north (d) Between 40 and 50 degrees north

173. Name the treeless low-lying and mostly level areas found in the northern edges of Europe, Asia and North America:

(a) Moorland (b) Tundra (c) Grasslands (d) Taiga

174. Name the rolling treeless habitat on high ground which was once covered mainly with pine forests and is found on the southern edge of the Tundra:

(a) Moorland (b) Tundra (c) Grasslands (d) Taiga

175. In what type of habitat are the biotic communities that once lived in the Ice Age found?

(a) Tundra (b) Moorland (c) Both the above (d) That kind of habitat are no longer to be found

176. Grasslands are known by different names in various parts of the world, such as Veldt in South Africa, Savannah in East Africa, Prairie in North America, Pampas in South America and Meadow in Europe. What is the name given to Central Asian grasslands?

(a) Chalk downland (b) Steppe (c) Semi-arid grassland (d) Prairie

177. What is the most important artificially induced recurring phenomenon in the grasslands?

(a) Fire damages (b) Grass cutting (c) Animals (d) Pesticides

178. What is the most preferred habitat for the giraffe (*Giraffa camelopardalis*) and the African elephant (*Loxodonta africana*)?

(a) Savannah (b) Rain forest (c) Desert (d) Veldt

179. Communal grazing by herbivores in mixed herds in the vast grasslands offers an advantage. What is it?

(a) Predator avoidance for survival (b) Preferred feeding on various types of plants thus full use of habitat (c) Both the above (d) None of the above

180. Name the largest animal inhabiting the pampas of South America:

(a) Pampas Deer (*Blastoceros campestris*) (b) Rhea (*Rhea americana*) (c) Giraffe (*Giraffa camelopardalis*) (d) Cheetal (*Axis axis*)

181. Name the largest South American grassland mammal:

(a) Pampas Deer (*Blastoceros campestris*) (b) Rhea (*Rhea americana*) (c) Giraffe (*Giraffa camelopardalis*) (d) Cheetal (*Axis axis*)

182. Most grasslands of the world are threatened with desertification, over-grazing, over-cultivation and urbanization. What is the most sound management strategy to meet these problems?

(a) Reducing the biotic pressure (b) Developing high-yielding agriculture (c) Maintenance of wild grass gene pool for cereal breeding (d) All the above

183. Which lake is an important breeding area for the California gulls and a critical stopover for the Wilson's phalarope?

(a) Chilka Lake (b) Pichhola Lake (c) Mono Lake (d) Jaisamand Lake

184. What is the adaptation in the mountain-dwelling wild animals to counteract low temperatures?

(a) Thick and hairy coat, short ears, nose and tail to minimise heat loss (b) Low body temperature (c) Thick blood (d) Short head

185. What is the adaptation in the blood of the mountain-dwelling animals to cope up with low oxygen?

(a) More red blood corpuscles (b) More white blood corpuscles

186. What is the most important ecological function of the wetlands?

(a) Spawning nurseries for fish breeding (b) Productive ecosystems supporting various food chains (c) Groundwater recharge (d) All the above

187. Name the largest freshwater lake in the world:

(a) Wular (b) Lake Superior (c) Lake Baikal (d) Black Sea

188. Which is deepest lake in the world?

(a) Wular (b) Lake Superior (c) Lake Baikal (d) Black Sea

189. What is the percentage of endemism in the 1200 animal and 500 plant species recorded in Lake Baikal?

(a) 50 (b) 60 (c) 70 (d) 80

190. What is the characteristic of the Pleistocene refugia?

(a) High biotic diversity (b) Few species per unit area (c) No ecologic resource available (d) Rich in shrubs

191. What are the characteristics of animals found in islands?

(a) Large body-size due to less competition for food and very few predators, hence poor defence mechanism (b) Small body-size (c) Short nose (d) Elongated tail

192. What is the reason for the extinction of the dodo (*Raphus cucullatus*) in Mauritius?

(a) Defencelessness as a result of heavy body and flightlessness (b) Racial senescence (c) Predation (d) Capture for trade

193. What activity threatens the coastal wildlife?

(a) Pollution due to oil spills, sewage, industrial disposal, waste-dumping and construction (b) Plantation (c) Fishing (d) Boating

194. What is the primary source of food for marine animal life?

(a) Phytoplankton (b) Zooplankton (c) Seaweed (d) Grass

195. Reefs, says Mark Carwarding, may be described as tropical forests under the sea and support a variety of wildlife. What is the main threat to the reefs of the world?

(a) Pollution and mining (b) Boating (c) Natural senescence (d) Fishing

196. Identify the major spawning areas and fish nurseries of the world:

(a) Mangrove swamps and estuaries (b) Rivers (c) Deep oceans (d) Ponds

197. Identify the activities threatening our marine environment:

(a) Reef destruction, pollution and over-exploitation of living resources (b) Shore plantation (c) Boating (d) All the above

198. Which tree, yielding a malarial drug, was depleted from its natural habitat in South America and seeds had to be propagated at the Royal Botanical Garden to help re-establish species in the wild?

(a) *Coffea* sp. (b) *Chinchona* sp. (c) *Penicillium* sp. (d) *Azadirachta* sp.

199. Which is the world's richest biological ecosystem?

(a) Wetlands (b) Tropical moist forests (c) Deserts (d) Grasslands

200. Name the world's largest forest area:

(a) Coniferous forests, Siberia (b) Rain forests, Amazonia (c) Dry deciduous forests, India (d) Thorn· forests, India

201. For what kind of forests is Amazonia famous?

(a) Coniferous forests (b) Rain forests (c) Dry deciduous forests (d) Thorn forests

202. How many biogeographical realms are recognized by M.D.F. Udvardy in the world?

(a) 5 (b) 6 (c) 7 (d) 8

203. How many biomes are recognized by M.D.F. Udvardy in the world?

(a) 5 (b) 8 (c) 9 (d) 14

204. In which biogeographical realm does India fall?

(a) Nearctic realm (b) Neotropical realm (c) Palearctic realm (d) Indo-Malayan realm

205. In which biogeographical realm do most parts of North America fall?

(a) Nearctic realm (b) Neotropical realm
(c) Palearctic realm (d) Oceanian realm

206. In which biogeographical realm does South America fall?
(a) Nearctic realm (b) Neotropical realm
(c) Palearctic realm (d) Oceanian realm

207. In which biogeographical realm do most parts of the Asian continent fall?
(a) Nearctic realm (b) Neotropical realm
(c) Palearctic realm (d) Oceanian realm

208. In which biogeographical realm does most of the African continent fall?
(a) Afrotropical realm (b) Palearctic realm
(c) Australian realm (d) Nearctic realm

209. In which biogeographical realm do the northern parts of the African continent fall?
(a) Afrotropical realm (b) Palearctic realm
(c) Australian realm (d) Nearctic realm

210. In which biogeographical realm does Australia fall?
(a) Afrotropical realm (b) Palearctic realm
(c) Australian realm (d) Nearctic realm

211. To which biogeographical realm is the WWF-Andean Conservation Programme related?
(a) Afrotropical (b) Indo-Malayan
(c) Nearctic (d) Neotropical

212. The Cape Floristic Kingdom of South Africa harbours the richest collection of plant species in the world. What is the species density per ten square km. in the region?
(a) 400 (b) 800 (c) 1100 (d) 1300

5
THE PLANTS

213. Which plant yields *cocaine?*

(a) *Cinchona* (b) *Calvaria major* (c) *Erythroxylon coca* (d) *Azadirachta indica*

214. Which tree yields natural chewing gum?

(a) Chile Tree (*Manilkara zapota*) (b) Katira (*Sterculia urens*) (c) Bija (*Pterocarpus marsupium*) (d) Neem (*Azadirachta indica*)

215. Name an endemic pine of the Himalayas which yields the chilgoza of commerce:

(a) *Pinus wallichiana* (b) *P. excelsa* (c) *P. pinaster* (d) *P. gerardiana*

216. The flower of which plant yields the saffron of commerce?

(a) *Cassia fistula* (b) *Mesua ferrea* (c) *Viola odorata* (d) *Crocus sativus*

217. Which of the following trees are depleted in the wild as a result of logging and habitat destruction?

(a) Red Cedar (*Toona australis*), Australia (b) White Pine *(Pinus strobus)*, North America (c) Coffinwood (*Taiwania cryptomerioides*), China (d) All the above

218. Which Asian country became the first in the world in 1980 to establish a ministry for indigenous medicines and medicinal plants?

(a) India (b) Nepal (c) Bhutan (d) Sri Lanka

219. What do you mean by 'commercial extinction' of a species?

(a) Depletion of species in the wild due to over-exploitation (b) Species totally wiped off from the natural habitat (c) Species unable to reproduce in the wild (d) Species producing infertile seeds

220. When coffee plantations in Brazil, derived from a single variety, were damaged due to Leaf Rust disease, which continent supplied wild genetic resource to breed a new resistant variety?

(a) Asia (b) Europe (c) Australia (d) Africa

221. Which plant yields the 'Golden fruit of the Andes'?

(a) Saguaro (*Cereus giganteus*) (b) Mexican yam (*Dioscorea composita*) (c) Naranjilla (*Solanum quitoense*) (d) Chilgoza (*Pinus gerardiana*)

222. Which is the largest cactus in the world?

(a) Saguaro (*Cereus giganteus*) (b) Mexican yam (*Dioscorea composita*) (c) Naranjilla (*Solanum quitoense*) (d) Chilgoza (*Pinus gerardiana*)

223. From which species are birth control pills prepared?

(a) Saguaro (*Cereus giganteus*) (b) Mexican yam (*Dioscorea composita*) (c) Naranjilla (*Solanum quitoense*) (d) Chilgoza (*Pinus gerardiana*)

224. Name the tree which yields a sap used as milk by Venezuelans?

(a) *Brosimum utile* (b) *Protea repens* (c) *Oryza nivara* (d) *Ficus elastica*

225. Name the national flower of South Africa?

(a) *Brosimum utile* (b) *Protea repens* (c) *Oryza nivara* (d) *Ficus elastica*

226. In the year 1954 the oldest known living seed was found in frozen silt in Canada. Its estimated age was 10,000 years. Name it:

(a) Pitcher plant (*Nepenthes rajah*) (b) Arctic Lupin (*Lupinus arcticus*) (c) Pummelo (*Citrus maxima*) (d) Saffron (*Crocus sativus*)

227. Which is the biggest pitcher plant having a two-litre capacity pitcher?

(a) *Nepenthes khasiana* (b) *N. rajah* (c) *N. alba* (d) (a) & (b) are synonyms

228. Which country has the maximum number of orchids in the world?

(a) Bhutan (b) Canada (c) Zaire (d) Colombia

229. Which tree yields the heaviest wood in the world?

(a) Black Iron Wood (*Olea laurifolia*) (b) Balsa (*Ochroma pyramidale*) (c) Durian (*Durio zibethinus*) (d) Coconut (*Cocos nucifera*)

230. Name the largest seed in plant kingdom:

(a) Coco De Mer (*Lodoicea maldivica*) (b) Wax Palm (*Ceroxylon quinuense*) (c) Coconut (*Cocos nucifera*) (d) Balsa (*Ochroma pyramidale*)

231. Which is the most delicious fruit in the world?

(a) Black Iron Wood (*Olea laurifolia*) (b) Balsa (*Ochroma pyramidale*) (c) Durian (*Durio zibethinus*) (d) Coconut (*Cocus nucifera*)

232. Which is the national tree of Colombia?

(a) Coco De Mer (*Lodoicea maldivica*) (b) Wax Palm (*Ceroxylon quinuense*) (c) Coconut (*Cocos nucifera*) (d) Balsa (*Ochroma pyramidale*)

233. Which is the tallest palm on earth?

(a) Coco De Mer (*Lodoicea maldivica*) (b) Wax Palm (*Ceroxylon quinuense*) (c) Coconut (*Cocos nucifera*) (d) Balsa (*Ochroma pyramidale*)

234. Which is the largest flower in the world?

(a) Rafflesia (*Rafflesis arnoldii*) (b) Bristle Cone Pine (*Pinus longaeva*) (c) Giant Sequoia (*Sequoiadendron giganteum*) (d) Coast Redwood (*Sequoia sempervirens*)

235. Which is the oldest tree alive today?

(a) Rafflesia (*Rafflesis arnoldii*) (b) Bristle Cone Pine (*Pinus longaeva* (c) Giant Sequoia (*Sequoiadendron giganteum*) (d) Coast Redwood (*Sequoia sempervirens*)

236. Which is the most massive tree in the world?

(a) Rafflesia (*Rafflesis arnoldii*) (b) Bristle Cone Pine (*Pinus longaeva*) (c) Giant Sequoia (*Sequoiadendron giganteum*) (d) Coast Redwood (*Sequoia sempervirens*)

237. Which is the tallest tree in the world?

(a) Coast Redwood (*Sequoia sempervirens*) (b) Montezuma Cypress (*Taxodium mucronatum*) (c) Bristle Cone Pine (*Pinus longaeva*) (d) Giant Sequoia (*Sequoiadendron giganteum*)

238. Which tree has the maximum girth in the world?

(a) Coast Redwood (*Sequoia sempervirens*) (b) Montezuma Cypress (*Taxodium mucronatum*) (c) Bristle Cone Pine (*Pinus longaeva*) (d) Giant Sequoia (*Sequoiadendron giganteum*)

239. Name a living fossil tree considered to have become extinct about twenty million years ago, which was discovered in 1941 in China?

(a) Chilgoza (*Pinus gerardiana*) (b) Maidenhair Tree (*Ginkgo biloba*) (c) Dawn Redwood (*Metasequoia glyptostroboides*) (d) Montezuma Cypress (*Taxodium mucronatum*)

240. How many species of *Carnivorous plants* are found in the world?

(a) 200 (b) 400 (c) 415 (d) 450

241. Name the plant producing the largest infloresence in the world:
    (a) Chilgoza Pine (*Pinus gerardiana*)
    (b) Branching Palm (*Hyphaene dichotoma*)
    (c) Talipot Palm (*Corypha umbraculifera*)
    (d) Thorny Bamboo (*Bambusa arundinacea*)

242. What was the main source of food in the ancient civilizations of Mesopotamia, Egypt, Greece and Rome?
    (a) Wheat (b) Rice (c) Maize (d) Sesame

243. What was the staple food of the ancient civilizations of the Inca, Aztec and Maya in the Americas?
    (a) Wheat (b) Rice (c) Maize (d) Sesame

244. What was the staple food of the ancient civilizations in India, China and Japan?
    (a) Wheat (b) Rice (c) Maize (d) Sesame

245. Which is the tallest recorded bamboo in the world?
    (a) Thorny Bamboo (*Bambusa arundinacea*)
    (b) Muli Bamboo (*Melocana bambusoides*)
    (c) Golden Bamboo (*Bambusa vulgaris*)
    (d) Solid Bamboo (*Dendrocalamus strictus*)

246. What are the Vavilov centres?
    (a) Centres of diversity of wild relatives of crop plants (b) Centres of diversity of wild relatives of domestic animals (c) Both above (d) None of the above

247. What is the estimated number of potential edible plant species in the world?
    (a) 80,000 (b) 100,000 (c) 200,000 (d) 30,000

248. How many species of plants are cultivated to meet more than 80 per cent food requirements of the world?

(a) 10 (b) 13 (c) 15 (d) 20

249. In which locality is the rarest pitcher plant *Napenthes rajah* found?

(a) Mount Kinabalu, Sabah (b) Himalayas, India (c) Kilmanjaro, Tanzania (d) All above

6

THE MAMMALS

250. Which continent is known as the 'Paradise of big game'?

(a) Asia (b) South America (c) Australia (d) Africa

251. Africa is particularly famous for antelopes and gazelles. How many species of deer are found in Africa?

(a) 10 (b) 9 (c) 5 (d) 4

252. Which country has the highest number of deer species in the world?

(a) India (b) South Africa (c) Bhutan (d) Zaire

253. What is the number of endemic species of mammals in India?

(a) 5 (b) 10 (c) 15 (d) 21

254. Name the only antelope in the world with two pairs of horns:

(a) Black Buck (*Antilope cervicapra*)
(b) Chausingha (*Tetracerus quadricornis*)

(c) Chital (*Axis axis*) (d) Nilgai (*Boselaphus tragocamelus*)

255. What is the number of toes evident in the footprint of the rhinoceros?

(a) 1 (b) 2 (c) 3 (d) 4

256. What is the typical habitat of the moose (*Alces alces*) and red deer (*Cervus elaphus*)?

(a) Tropical rain forests (b) Temperate forests (c) Coniferous forests (d) Deserts

257. Almost all Javan rhinoceros are contained in Ujong Kulon National Park in Indonesia. What is the recommendation of the Asian Rhino Specialist Group of the Species Survival Commission of the IUCN to save this species from extinction?

(a) Translocation of animals to establish an alternative population (b) Captive breeding (c) Food provisioning (d) All the above

258. Name an animal of the cat family found in the region from Mexico to southern Brazil, that has monkey-like climbing skills and is endangered because of being hunted for its coat and loss of habitat by deforestation:

(a) Asiatic lion (*Panthera leo persica*) (b) African lion (*P.l. leo*) (c) Margay (*Felis wiedi*) (d) Tiger (*Panthera tigris*)

259. In which year was the Golden Bamboo Lemur (*Hapalemur aureus*) discovered and identified?

(a) 1980 (b) 1982 (c) 1984 (d) 1986

260. What is the source of threat to the survival of Margay (*Felis wiedi*)?

(a) Hunting for its fur (b) Hunting for oil (c) Hunting for its bone (d) Hunting for its claws

261. In which locality is the Golden Bamboo Lemur (*Hepalemur aureus*) discovered and identified?

(a) Bhutan (b) Madagascar (c) China (d) Uganda

262. The first white tigress to leave India and to reach U.S.A. was one purchased by Radio Corporation of America from the Maharaja of Rewa in the year 1960. Name it:

(a) Mohini (b) Mohan (c) Suketi (d) Nandan

263. Name the earliest known document in which the white tiger is mentioned:

(a) Ramayana (b) Gita (c) Mahabharata (d) Akbarnama

264. Which zoological park has the largest collection of white tigers in India?

(a) Sanjay Gandhi Biological Park, Patna (b) Nandankanan Biological Park, Bhubaneswar (c) Nehru Zoological Park, Hyderabad (d) Arignar Anna Zoological Park, Madras

265. Name the location of the largest collection (28 in the year 1990) of white tigers in the world:

(a) Hawthorne Circus of Illinois (b) Nandankanan Biological Park of India (c) Ex-Maharaja of Rewa (d) Ex-Maharaja of Bharatpur

266. Name the largest primate in the world:

(a) Orangutan (*Pongo pygmaeus*) (b) Mountain Gorilla (*Gorilla gorilla*) (c) Pileated Gibbon

(Hylobates pileatus) (d) Red Colobus *(Colobus kirkii)*

267. Name the largest primate of the Asian continent:

(a) Orangutan *(Pongo pygmaeus)* (b) Mountain Gorilla *(Gorilla gorilla)* (c) Pileated Gibbon *(Hylobates pileatus)* (d) Red Colobus *(Colobus kirkii)*

268. Name the primate for which the Tanzanian Government established the Jozani Forest Reserve in Zanzibar Island to protect the sole habitat of the species:

(a) Red Colobus *(Colobus kirkii)* (b) Golden Lion Tamarin *(Leontopithecus rosalia)* (c) Red Uakari *(Cacajao rubicundus)* (d) Orangutan *(Pongo pygmaeus)*

269. Which type of teeth in pigs are seen as tusks?

(a) Canines in the upper jaw (b) Molars in the upper jaw (c) Canines in the lower jaw (d) Molars in the lower jaw

270. In which country are the Woolly Spider Monkey *(Brachyteles arachnoides)*, the Golden Lion Tamarin *(Leontopithecus rosalia)*, the Whitenosed Saki *(Chiropotes albinasus)* found?

(a) India (b) Tanzania (c) Peru (d) Brazil

271. Name the smallest primate in the world:

(a) Lesser Mouse-Lemur *(Microcebus murinus)*
(b) Red Ruffed Lemur *(Lemur variegatus ruber)*
(c) Aye-aye *(Daubentonia madagascariensis)*
(d) Golden Lion Tamarin *(Brachyteles arachnoides)*

272. Name the most primitive primate in the world:

(a) Red Ukari (*Cacaiao rubicundus*) (b) Red Colobus (*Colobus kirkii*) (c) Aye-aye (*Daubentonia madagascariensis*) (d) Gorilla (*Gorilla gorilla*)

273. Which is the smallest wild cat in the world?

(a) Spanish Lynx (*Felis lynx pardina*), Spain (b) Black-footed Cat (*Felis nigripes*), South Africa (c) Northern Kit Fox (*Vulpes velox hebes*), U.S.A. (d) Rustyspotted Cat (*Felis rubiginosa*), India

274. Name the unique animal that combines the features of the cats, civets and mongooses?

(a) Fossa (*Cryptoprocta ferox*) (b) Black-footed Ferret (*Mustela nigripes*) (c) Otter Civet (*Cynogale bennetti*) (d) Lynx (*Eelis lynx*)

275. Which animal is known variously as Puma, Panther or Mountain Lion?

(a) Cougar (*Felis concolor*) (b) Jaguar (*Panthera onca*) (c) Leopard (*Panthera pardus*) (d) Cheetah (*Acinonyx jubatus*)

276. Name the largest cat of the North and South America:

(a) Cougar (*Felis concolor*) (b) Jaguar (*Panthera onca*) (c) Leopard (*Panthera pardus*) (d) None of the above

277. In which mountain range is the Spectacled Bear (*Tremarctos ornatus*) found?

(a) Himalayas (b) Alps (c) Satpuras (d) Andes

278. In which country is the Giant Panda (*Ailuropoda melanoleuca*) found?

(a) Japan (b) India (c) Nepal (d) China

279. Name the only member of the dog family that thrives on insects:

(a) Leopard cat (*Felis bengalensis*) (b) Bat-eared fox (*Otocyon megalotis*) (c) Indian Wild Dog (*Cuon alpinus*) (d) Grey Wolf (*Canis lupus*)

280. Which primate is famous for its 'Chest-beating display'?

(a) Gorilla (*Gorilla gorilla*) (b) Gibbon (*Hylobates* sp.) (c) Tarsius (*Tarsius* sp.) (d) Colobus (*Colobus* sp.)

281. How many races of the gorilla are found in the world?

(a) 6 (b) 5 (c) 4 (d) 3

282. Where is the gorilla found?

(a) Asia (b) Central Africa (c) Australia (d) U.S.A.

283. In which species of primate, do individuals build a new nest every evening to sleep during the night?

(a) Gorilla (*Gorilla gorilla*) (b) Hollock Gibbon (*Hylobates hoolock*) (c) Golden Langur (*Presbytis geei*) (d) Red Colobus (*Colobus kirkii*)

284. What is the food habit of the gorilla (*Gorilla gorilla*)?

(a) Herbivorous (b) Carnivorous (c) Omnivorous (d) Capriphagous

285. What is the Koala (*Phascolarctos cinereus*)?

(a) Bear (b) Frog (c) Snake (d) Marsupial

286. Name the only cat that does not have retractable claws:

(a) Lion (*Panthera leo*) (b) Cheetah (*Acinonyx jubatus*) (c) Leopard (*Panthera pardus*) (d) Tiger (*Panthera tigris*)

287. What is the food of the Koala (*Phascolarctos cinereus*)?

(a) Neem leaves (b) Babul leaves (c) Eucalyptus leaves (d) Acacia leaves

288. How many species of the chipmunk are found in the world?

    (a) 15 (b) 20 (c) 21 (d) 22

289. How many species of the chipmunk are found in Asia?

    (a) 1 (b) 2 (c) 3 (d) 4

290. To which group of mammals does the chipmunk belong?

    (a) Cat (b) Rodent (c) Bat (d) Dog

291. What is a collection of the wolf (*Canis lupus*) called?

    (a) Herd (b) Flock (c) Pride (d) Pack

292. Which animal has the widest natural range of distribution of any living land mammal?

    (a) Grey Wolf (*Canis lupus*) (b) European Beaver (*Castor fiber*) (c) European Wild Cat (*Felis sylvestris*) (d) Tiger (*Panthera tigris*)

293. The period of sexual motivation and ill temper in the male Asian elephants is called *musth*. Recent findings suggest that African elephants also experience a similar seasonal fluctuation, accompanied by a characteristic greenish coloured dangling and dribbling penis. What is the phenomenon called?

    (a) Musth (b) Green penis syndrome (c) Hasth (d) Sexual syndrome

294. Name the largest hare in the world:

    (a) European Beaver (*Castor fiber*) (b) Lynx (*Felis lynx*) (c) Antelope Jackrabbit (*Lepus alleni*) (d) Black-naped Hare (*Lepus nigricollis*)

295. What is the nest of a rabbit or hare called?

(a) Lodge (b) Home (c) Farm (d) Form

296. What is the food of the antelope jackrabbit (*Lepus alleni*)?

(a) Cacti, grasses and herbs (b) Bats (c) Fruits

297. Normally the typical rabbit is adapted for burrowing and the hare for running. Name the animal from this group which is equally adapted for both:

(a) Black-naped Hare (*Lepus nigricollis*) (b) Antelope Jackrabbit (*Lepus alleni*) (c) Varying Hare (*Lepus americanus*) (d) Himalayan Mouse Hare (*Ochotoma roylei*)

298. How many quills are found on the body of a porcupine?

(a) 500 (b) 30,000 (c) 50,000 (d) 60,000

299. How many species of porcupine are found in the world?

(a) 5 (b) 10 (c) 15 (d) 20

300. Where is the Spanish Lynx (*Felis pardina*) found?

(a) Iberian Peninsula and Guadalquivir Delta (b) Canary Islands (c) Balearic Islands

301. Which is the largest marsupial in the world?

(a) Koala (*Phascolarctos cinereus*) (b) Red Kangaroo (*Macropus rufus*) (c) Grey Kangaroo (*Macropus canguru*) (d) Yak (*Bos grunnies*)

302. What is the weight of a newborn red kangaroo (*Macropus rufus*)?

(a) 4 grams (b) 2 grams (c) 3 grams (d) 1 gram

303. What is the food of the kangaroo?

(a) Grass and plants (b) Rodents (c) Nuts (d) Birds

304. What is the young kangaroo called?
    (a) Pup (b) Cub (c) Calf (d) Joey
305. Where are the kangaroos found?
    (a) Asia (b) Australia (c) Africa (d) South America
306. What is the colour of the coat of the 'varying hare' (*Lepus americanus mcfarlanii*) during winters?
    (a) White (b) Black (c) Brown (d) Green
307. What is the colour of the coat of stoat or short-tailed weasel (*Mustela erminea*) during winters?
    (a) White (b) Black (c) Brown (d) Green
308. What adaptation do animals living in the tundra and moorland make to avoid the potential predators during winters?
    (a) Moulting into white pelt (b) Burrowing (c) Moulting into black pelt (d) Moulting into brown pelt
309. How many species of squirrel are found in the world?
    (a) 15 (b) 50 (c) 100 (d) 270
310. Name the species with the longest hair in the world:
    (a) Musk Ox (*Ovibos moschatus*) (b) Asiatic Wild Buffalo (*Bubalus bubalis*) (c) Yak (*Bos grunnies*) (d) Lion (*Panthera leo*)
311. What is the distribution and habitat of the musk ox (*Ovibos moschatus*) ?
    (a) Arctic tundra (b) Antarctica (c) Africa (d) India
312. Name the animal that looks like a cross between a dog, a bear and a weasel:

(a) Echidna (*Tachyglossus aculeatus*) (b) Norway Lemming (*Lemus lemus*) (c) Wolverine (*Gulo gulo*) (d) American Bison (*Bison bison*)

313. What is the food of the echidna (*Tachyglossus aculeatus*)?

    (a) Termites and ants (b) Fruits (c) Leaves (d) Roots

314. In the year 1700, before the white settlers arrived, North American prairies sustained more than 60 million American bisons (*Bison bison*). But around the year 1900, bisons were hunted to extinction in the wild and managed to survive only in captivity. Captive bred animals have since been released in the wild. What is the estimated number in the wild today?

    (a) 50 (b) 500 (c) 5,000 (d) 50,000

315. Name the fastest land mammal in the world:

    (a) Tiger (*Panthera tigris*) (b) Cheetah (*Acinonyx jubatus*) (c) Lion (*Panthera leo*) (d) Black buck (*Antilope cervicapra*)

316. How many races of tiger (*Panthera tigris*) are recognized in the world?

    (a) 5 (b) 6 (c) 7 (d) 8

317. What is the place of origin of the tiger?

    (a) Siberia (b) India (c) Java (d) Kenya

318. How many races of tigers are considered extinct?

    (a) 1 (b) 3 (c) 4 (d) 7

319. Which of the following races of tiger is extinct?

    (a) Caspian Tiger (*Panthera tigris virgata*) (b) Bali Tiger (*Panthera tigris baltica*) (c) Javan

Tiger (*Panthera tigris sendiacus*) (d) All of the above

320. Which carnivorous mammal was tamed by Indian princes for sport hunting?
(a) Lion (*Panthera leo*) (b) Panther (*Panthera pardus*) (c) Cheetah (*Acinonyx jubatus*) (d) Tiger (*Panthera tigris*)

321. What is the offspring of a cross between a lion and a tigress called?
(a) Tigon (b) Liger (c) Litigon (d) Ligon

322. What is the offspring of a cross between a tiger and a lioness called?
(a) Tigon (b) Liger (c) Litigon (d) Ligon

323. What is the cross between a tigon and a lion called?
(a) Tigon (b) Liger (c) Litigon (d) Ligon

324. Which cat has a pelt colour pattern like a panther?
(a) Lynx (*Felis lynx*) (b) Caracal (*Felis caracal*) (c) Leopard cat (*Felis bengalensis*) (d) Lion (*Panthera leo*)

325. What method is used for estimating the tiger population in the wild?
(a) Pugmark census (b) Facemark census (c) Direct visual count (d) Waterhole count

326. Which is the largest land mammal in the world?
(a) Asian Elephant (*Elaphas maximus*) (b) African Elephant (*Loxodonta africana*) (c) Gaur (*Bos gaurus*) (d) Indian Onehorned Rhino (*Rhinoceros unicornis*)

327. What is the elephant tusk?

(a) **Modified incisor** (b) **Modified molar**
(c) **Modified premolar**

328. What is the length of the longest recorded tusk from an African elephant (*Loxodonta africana*)?

    (a) 299 cm (b) 336 cm

329 What is the length of the longest recorded tusk from an Asian elephant (*Elephas maximus*)?

    (a) 299 cm (b) 336 cm (c) 350 cm (d) 400 cm

330. The Asian elephant (*Elephas maximus*) has four nails on its hindfoot. How many does the African elephant (*Loxodonta africana*) have?

    (a) 3 (b) 4 (c) 5 (d) 6

331. Many species of the bandicoot from the arid and semi-arid zones of Australia have either become extinct or are facing extinction. Why?

    (a) Competition with cattle, sheep and rabbit for food and habitat (b) Predation by introduced cats and foxes (c) Both the above

332. Which is the most abundant species of seal in the world?

    (a) Leopard Seal (*Hydruga leptonyx*)
    (b) Crabeater Seal (*Lobodon carcinophagus*)
    (c) Elephant Seal (*Mirounga leonia* and *M. anguistirostris*) (d) Weddel Seal (*Leptonychotes weddilli*)

333. The weddel seal (*Leptonychotes weddilli*) is the deepest diver of all seals descending up to zoom. How long can it stay submerged?

    (a) Four hours (b) Three hours (c) Two hours (d) One hour

334. What is the offspring of a seal called?

(a) Joey (b) Cub (c) Calf (d) Pup

335. Which is the largest land predator in the world?

(a) Tiger (*Panthera tigris*) (b) Polar Bear (*Ursus maritimus*) (c) Lion (*Panthera leo*) (d) Leopard Seal (*Hydruga leptonyx*)

336. What is the body size of the adult polar bear (*Ursus maritimus*)?

(a) Shoulder height 1.6 M, weight 800 Kg.
(b) Shoulder height 2.5 M, weight 1000 Kg.
(c) Shoulder height 1.0 M, weight 400 Kg.
(d) Shoulder height 1.0 M, weight 100 Kg.

337. What is the region-wise distributional range of the polar bear (*Ursus maritimus*)?

(a) Arctic circle (b) Antarctica (c) Southern Hemisphere (d) Northern Hemisphere

338. What is the estimated size of the polar bear population in the world?

(a) 400 (b) 500 (c) 10,000 (d) 20,000

339. Which is the mammal known to dwell in the highest altitudes, often seen at 6000 m, in the world?

(a) Yak (*Bos mutus*) (b) Chamois (*Rupicapra rupicapra*) (c) African Klipspringer (*Oreotrogus oreotragus*) (d) Gaur (*Bos gaurus*)

340. Which animal is the official symbol of the World Wide Fund for Nature?

(a) Giant Panda (*Ailuropoda melanoleuca*) (b) Red Panda (*Ailuros fulgens*) (c) Yak (*Bos mutus*) (d) Chamois (*Rupicapra rupicapra*)

341. Which is the most northerly living macaque on earth?

    (a) Japanese Macaque (*Macaca fuscata*)
    (b) Pigtailed Macaque (*M. nemestrina*)
    (c) Stumptailed Macaque (*M. arctoides*)
    (d) Longtailed Macaque (*M. fasciacularis*)

342. Name the largest rodent in the world:

    (a) Capybara (*Hydrochaerus hydrochaeris*)
    (b) Arctic Ground Squirrel (*Citellus undulatus*)
    (c) Palm Squirrel (*Funambulus palmarum*)
    (d) Common Giant Flying Squirrel (*Eupetaurus cinereus*)

343. The proboscis monkey (*Nasalis larvatus*) is called the 'elephant of the monkey world', for it has a nose more than seven centimeters long. Where is it found?

    (a) Bermuda (b) Borneo (c) Brazil (d) India

344. The Grevy's Zebra (*Equus grevyi*) and Burchell's Zebra (*Equus burchelli*) have differing coat strips. Grevy's Zebra has narrower stripes. What is the other difference?

    (a) Grevy's Zebra has larger ear pinna
    (b) Burchell's Zebra has larger ear pinna
    (c) Grevy's Zebra has splayed hooves (d) Both (a) and (c)

345. Name the only sea mammal that lacks thick blubber:

    (a) Blue Whale (*Balaenoptera musculus*)
    (b) Sperm Whale (*Physeter catodon*) (c) Sea Otter (*Enhydra lutris*) (d) Killer Whale (*Orcinus orca*)

346. Which mammal produces the largest litter — thirty-two young ones — in the world?

    (a) Virginian Opossum (*Didelphys marsupialis*)
    (b) Madagascar Tenrec (*Centetes ecaudatus*)

(c) *Microtus* mouse (d) Grant's Gazelle (*Gazella granti*)

347. Africa, the paradise of big game, has tne big five: elephant, rhinoceros, buffalo, giraffe and hippopotamus. How many of these are represented in India?

(a) Elephant, Rhinoceros, Buffalo (b) Rhinoceros and Giraffe (c) Giraffe, Hippopotamus (d) All the above

348. Name the only country where both the lion (*Panthera leo*) and the tiger (*Panthera tigris*) are found in the wild:

(a) Kenya (b) Pakistan (c) Uganda (d) India

349. Which Indian animal resembles the Thomson's gazelle of East Africa in size, appearance and habitat requirements?

(a) Chinkara (*Gazella gazella*) (b) Blackbuck (*Antilope cervicapra*) (c) Chital (*Axis axis*) (d) Nilgai (*Boselaphus tragocamelus*)

350. Which animal in Africa is called the 'King of the Beasts'?

(a) Lion (*Panthera leo*) (b) Cheetah (*Acinonyx jubatus*) (c) Leopard (*Panthera pardus*) (d) Tiger (*Panthera tigris*)

351. Four species of primates share characteristics close to man's : presence of two nipples, absence of tail and presence of five digits, with one opposable thumb, on both hands and feet. One of these is man himself. Name the other animals:

(a) Chimpanzee (*Pan troglodytes*) (b) Orangutan (*Pongo pygmeus*) (c) Gorilla (*Gorilla gorilla*) (d) All above

54

352. The easiest way to save a species from extinction is to stop commercial exploitation. Name an antelope from Russia which was protected in 1919 against hunting and is now the most abundant wild ungulate of the country, numbering around three million. Following this, it is hunted now to provide a sustained supply of hides, meat and industrial fat:

(a) Saiga Antelope (*Saiga tatarica*) (b) Pronghorn Antelope (*Antilocapra americana*) (c) Mountain Gazelle (*Gazelle gazelle*) (d) Vicuna (*Vicugna vicugna*)

353. Name the only antelope of the North and South America:

(a) Saiga Antelope (*Saiga tatarica*) (b) Pronghorn Antelope (*Antilocapra americana*) (c) Mountain Gazelle (*Gazelle gazelle*) (d) Vicuna (*Vicugna vicugna*)

354. Name a relative of the camel and the llama which was over-hunted for its fine wool, reducing its population to a mere 6000 in the 1960s. In 1967 Peru established the Pampa Galeras Reserve to protect the species and now its population has increased to more than a lakh throughout its range in Peru, Chile and Argentina:

(a) Vicuna (*Vicugna vicugna*) (b) Saiga Antelope (*Saiga tatarica*) (c) Pronghorn Antelope (*Antilocapra americana*) (d) Mustang (*Equus cabellus*)

355. The Prague and Munich zoos played a decisive role in saving a species from extinction, depleted in the wild and found

only at these zoos. There are plans to reintroduce the captive bred animal in its original mountainous range along the Chinese-Mongolian borders. Name the species:

(a) Saiga Antelope (*Saiga tatarica*) (b) Mustang (*Equus cabellus*) (c) Przewalski's Horse (*Equus ferus przewalskii*)

356. An animal was hunted to extinction in the year 1972 from its natural desert habitat in the Arabian Peninsula. However, some of these, bred in captivity, were pooled at Phoenix Zoo in Arizona, USA, and captive bred animals were later released back into the Jiddat al Harassis Desert in 1982. It is the first example of an animal extinct in the natural habitat being successfully reintroduced. Name this animal:

(a) Scimitar-horned Oryx (*Oryx tao*) (b) White Oryx (*Oryx leucoryx*) (c) Tule Elk (*Cervus nannodes*) (d) Cheetah (*Acinonyx jubatus*)

357. Name the only country where the tule elk (*Cervus nannodes*) is found in the wild:

(a) Uganda (b) Japan (c) Somalia (d) California

358. Which animal uses a stick as a tool, to extract termites for food from their nest?

(a) Chimpanzee (*Pan troglodytes*) (b) Orangutan (*Pongo pygmeus*) (c) Pangolin (*Manis crasicaudata*) (d) White Oryx (*Oryx leucoryx*)

359. In order of most ancient to most recent, categorise animals that took to air during evolution:

(a) Insects, Bats, Birds (b) Birds, Bats, Insects
(c) Insects, Birds, Bats (d) Bats, Birds, Insects

360. In most of the group hunting animals such
as the lions, wild dogs and wolves, one
member of the team reacts individually to
the movement of the prey, without role-
specialization; but in one species of the Ivory
Coast individual members of the team charge
as driver, blockers, chasers and ambusher to
facilitate effective hunting. Name this species:
(a) Olive Baboon (*Papio anubis*) (b) Chimpanzee *(Pan troglodytes)* (c) Tiger (*Panthera tigris*)
(d) Leopard (*Panthera pardus*)

361. Name the only species of cat which is a pack
hunter and lives in a close-knit group:
(a) Tiger (*Panthera tigris*) (b) Lion (*Panthera
leo*) (c) Leopard *(Panthera pardus)* (d) Cheetah
(*Acinonyx jubatus*)

362. Which is the smallest rhinoceros in the world?
(a) Sumatran Rhino (*Didermoceros sumatrensis*)
900 Kg, 140 cm (b) Javan Rhino (*Rhinoceros
sondiacus*) 1575 Kg, 150 cm (c) Black Rhino
(*Diceros bicornis*) 1350 Kg, 150 cm (d) White
Rhino (*Ceratotherium simum*)

363. What is the difference between the legs of
the spotted hyaena (*Crocuta crocuta*) and the
striped hyaena (*Hyaena hyaena*)?
(a) Striped hyaena has longer legs (b) Striped
hyaena has comparatively larger forefeet than
the hindfeet (c) Outer surface of the legs are
striped in the striped hyaena (d) All the above

364. What name has been given to the govern-
ment-sponsored anti-poaching programme to

save the black rhino (*Diceros bicornis*) in Zimbabwe?

(a) Operation Stronghold (b) Operation Rhino (c) Operation Bicornis (d) Operation Life

365. The population of the black rhino (*Diceros bicornis*) in Africa was estimated to be around 100,000 in 1960. It was reduced to 15,000 in 1980 due to poaching for its horn to feed the markets in North Yemen and the Far East. What is the estimated number of black rhinos surviving in 1990?

(a) 1000 (b) 2000 (c) 3000 (d) 4000

366. For what purpose is the rhino horn mainly used in North Yemen?

(a) Aphrodisiacal medicine (b) Dagger handles (c) Bullets (d) Food

367. As the rhino population dwindles, due to killing for horns, poachers have started killing hippos (*Hippopotamus amphibius*) for the substitute ivory. From which part of the body is it obtained?

(a) Leg Bones (b) Teeth (c) Horns (d) Ribs

368. What is the approximate cost of the rhino horn in illegal international markets?

(a) Rs.9,00,000 per Kg (b) Rs. 90,000 per Kg (c) Rs.9,000 per Kg

369. What name has been given to the anti-poaching programme to save the black rhino (*Diceros bicornis*) from extinction in Namibia?

(a) Operation Stronghold (b) Operation Bicornis (c) Operation Survival (d) Operation Life

370. A revolutionary but unpopular step is being taken to save the black rhino from eventual extinction in Namibia. What is the strategy followed?

(a) Tranquillizing and dehorning (b) Ranching of all rhinos (c) Keeping all rhinos in zoos (d) Keeping all rhinos in one park

371. What is the estimated duration for regeneration of horns in a dehorned rhino?

(a) 1 year (b) 2 years (c) 3 years (d) 4 years

372. As per the census in 1990, how many northern white rhino (*Ceratotherium simum cottoni*) are surviving in the wild?

(a) 5 (b) 10 (c) 15 (d) 26

373. The black rhino (*Diceros bicornis*) has a pointed upper lip while the white rhino (*Ceratotherium simum*) has a square mouth. What is the difference in the feeding habits of these animals:

(a) Black Rhino, Shrub browser (b) White Rhino, Grass grazer (c) Both above (d) None of the above

374. As per the census in 1990, what is the total number of surviving Asiatic lions (*Panthera leo persica*) in the wild?

(a) 106 (b) 184 (c) 200 (d) 284

375. Which is the largest deer in the world?

(a) Sambhar (*Cervus unicolor*) (b) Moose (*Alces alces*) (c) Cheetal (*Axis axis*) (d) Hog Deer (*Axis porcinus*)

376. Which animal has the biggest antlers in the world?

(a) Sambhar (*Cervus unicolor*) (b) Moose (*Alces alces*) (c) Cheetal (*Axis axis*) (d) Hog Deer (*Axis porcinus*)

377. What is the estimated number of the Asian elephant (*Elephas maximus*) surviving in the wild?

(a) 46,000 (b) 60,000 (c) 90,000

378. In Sweden as many as 150,000 permits are issued every year to shoot a particular animal. Name it:

(a) Red Deer (*Cervus elephus*) (b) Elk (*Alces alces*) (c) White-tailed Deer (*Odocoileus virginianus*) (d) Hog Deer (*Axis porcinus*)

379. American and Russian scientists are planning to resurrect the extinct woolly mammoth by extracting chromosomes from the frozen cells of a mammoth, transplanting it into an enucleated egg of a living relative and implanting the resultant embryo into the womb of a surrogate mother. Which living species is to be used for this — yet to start — experiment?

(a) Asian Elephant (*Elephas maximus*) (b) African Elephant (*Loxodonata africana)* (c) Indian Rhino (*Rhinoceros unicornis*) (d) Asiatic Wild Buffalo (*Bubalus bubalis*)

380. Which bat in Thailand has become endangered due to exploitation for tourist souvenirs?

(a) Kittis hog-nosed or Bumblebee Bat (*Craseonycteris thonglongya*) (b) Ghost Bat (*Macroderma gigas*) (c) Indiana Bat (*Myotis sodalis*) (d) Painted Bat (*Kerivoula picta*)

381. Which is the largest bat in Africa?

(a) Vampire (*Desmodus rotundus*) (b) Hammer-head Bat (*Hypsignathus monstrosus*) (c) Daubenton's Bat (*Leuconoe daubentonii*) (d) Indiana Bat (*Myotis sodalis*)

7

THE BIRDS

382. Fossils of the first creature resembling present-day birds was found in the Jurassic slate formation in Bavaria and combined the features of birds and lizards. Name it:

(a) *Archaeopterix lithographica* (b) *Anser anser* (c) *Hesperornis regalis* (d) *Ichthyornis victor*

383. Which of the following is a fossil bird?

(a) *Archaepterix* (b) *Hesperornix* (c) *Ichthyornis* (d) All the above

384. What is the distinguishing feature of birds?

(a) Feathers (b) Hollow bones and two legs (c) Warm-blooded (d) All the above

385. The base of the bill in birds is sometimes covered by a peculiar type of skin. What is it known?

(a) Cere (b) Bristle (c) Plumage (d) Quills

386. What is the name of the organ in the digestive system of birds used for grinding and pulverizing hard shells, seeds and grains?

(a) Caeca (b) Gizzard (c) Remiges (d) Pterylae

387. What is the sound-producing organ of a bird called?

(a) Syrinx (b) Larynx (c) Bronchial tube (d) Trachea

388. Name the earliest form of flight in birds?
(a) Soaring (b) Gliding (c) Flapping (d) Hovering

389. How does soaring differ from gliding in birds?
(a) Thermals help in soaring (b) Thermals help in gliding (c) No difference (d) Both (a) and (b)

390. What is the flight of birds involving sailing on outstretched and motionless wings called?
(a) Hovering (b) Flapping (c) Gliding (d) Flying

391. What kind of nests are prepared by quails and junglefowls?
(a) Tunnel nests (b) Cavity nests (c) Scraps on the ground, lined with grass (d) Twig nest

392. What kind of nests are prepared by crows, kites, doves, vultures, cormorants and storks?
(a) Scraps on the ground (b) Twig nest in tree-tops (c) Cavity nest in tree-trunks (d) Tunnel nest in river banks

393. What is the nest-site of barbets, hornbills, owls and ducks?
(a) Tree tops (b) Mud nest on the ground (c) Cavities in tree-trunk (d) Bare ground

394. Which of the following groups of birds are primary cavity nesters, excavating their own cavities?
(a) Woodpeckers (b) Parakeets (c) Barbets (d) All the above

395. Which of the following groups of birds are secondary cavity nesters, using cavities excavated by the primary cavity nesters?

(a) Hornbills (b) Owls (c) Mynas (d) All the above

396. What kind of nest is prepared by bee-eaters, kingfishers and the hoopoe?

    (a) Mud nest (b) Cavity nest (c) Tunnel nest in earth banks (d) Cup-shaped grass nest

397. What kind of nest is prepared by whistling thrushes, blackbirds, swallows and martins?

    (a) Mud nest (b) Grass nest (c) Twig nest (d) Leaf nest

398. Which bird prepares the pendant nest?

    (a) Weaver bird (b) Sunbird (c) Flowerpecker (d) All the above

399. What kind of nest does a tailor bird construct?

    (a) Pendant nest (b) Doomed nest (c) Nest in leaves stitched together (d) Mud nest

400. Cuckoos have a typical phenomenon; what is it?

    (a) Egg-eating (b) Elaborate nest (c) Nest Parasitism (d) Courtship display

401. For which region do the Indian birds show strong affinity?

    (a) Africa (b) Indochina (c) Both the above

402. Name the fastest flying bird on earth:

    (a) Peregrine Falcon (*Falco peregrinus*) (b) Golden Eagle (*Aquila chrysaetos*) (c) Sooty Falcon (*Falco concolor*) (d) Grey Shrike (*Lanius exubitor*)

403. Which group of birds has the most acute vision?

    (a) Ducks (b) Cranes (c) Birds of Prey (d) Pheasants

404. Name the only family of birds in which individuals hold bits of food in one foot and bite pieces off, as we eat a sandwich:

(a) Pigeons and Doves (*Columbidae*) (b) Owls (*Strigidae*) (c) Gulls and Terns (*Laridae*) (d) Parakeets (*Psittacidae*)

405. Which bird lives on the highest altitude?

(a) Alpine Chough (*Pyrrhocorax graculus*) (b) Redbilled Chough (*Pyrrhocorax pyrrhocorax*) (c) Raven (*Corvus corax*) (d) Golden Oriole (*Oriolus oriolus*)

406. How many species of birds are scientifically recorded in the world?

(a) 8,500 (b) 9,016 (c) 10,000 (d) 11,006

407. How many zoological orders of birds are found in the world?

(a) 20 (b) 25 (c) 26 (d) 27

408. What is the number of zoological families of birds in the world?

(a) 150 (b) 155 (c) 160 (d) 165

409. What is the excreta of seabirds called?

(a) Dung (b) Guano (c) Waste (d) Debris

410. How many species of Megapodes (*Megapodidae*) are found in the world?

(a) 2 (b) 4 (c) 9 (d) 10

411. In which group of birds are the legs encased within the body down to the ankle joint?

(a) Orioles (*Oriolidae*) (b) Divers (*Gavidae*) (c) Kingfisher (*Alcedinidae*) (d) Swifts (*Apodidae*)

412. Except the *Afropavo* of Africa, in which area are all the species of pheasants confined?

(a) Southeast Asia (b) Southwest Asia (c) South America (d) Sri Lanka

413. How many species of waterfowls are found in the world?

(a) 50 (b) 60 (c) 100 (d) 145

414. Which Indian duck, currently under threat of extinction, is being bred in captivity at Slimbridge, U.K., for subsequent release in the wild?

(a) Pinkheaded Duck (*Rhodonessa caryophyllacea*) (b) Whitewinged Wood Duck (*Cairina scutulata*) (c) Scaup Duck (*Aythya marila*) (d) Smew (*Mergus albellus*)

415. Which crane breeds on the borders of Indochina?

(a) Blacknecked Crane (*Grus nigricollis*) (b) Siberian Crane (*Grus leucogeranus*) (c) Common Crane (*Grus grus*) (d) Sarus Crane (*Grus antigone*)

416. Which is the world's tallest flying bird?

(a) Common Crane (*Grus grus*) (b) Sarus Crane (*Grus antigone*) (c) Siberian Crane (*Grus leucogeranus*) (d) Blacknecked Crane (*Grus nigricollis*)

417. How many species of cranes are found in the world?

(a) 5 (b) 10 (c) 11 (d) 14

418. To which country is the Sarus Crane (*Grus antigone*) endemic?

(a) India (b) U.S.A. (c) Nepal (d) Kenya

419. How many species of storks are found in the world?

(a) 16 (b) 17 (c) 18 (d) 20

420. How many species of Flammingoes are found in the world?

(a) 1 (b) 2 (c) 3 (d) 4

421. Which group of birds display 'bowing and beak-clattering' while changing duties at the nest?

(a) Stork (b) Crane (c) Duck (d) Goose

422. Which bird is called the 'Snakebird'?

(a) Little Cormorant (*Phalacrocorax niger*)
(b) Common Cormorant (*Phalacrocorax carbo*)
(c) Darter (*Anhinga rufa*) (d) Common Crane (*Grus grus*)

423. What is the feeding habit of the 'Snakebird' (*Anhinga rufa*)?

(a) Harpooning the snakes (b) Harpooning the fish (c) Snail-eating (d) Fruit-eating

424. How many species of penguins (*Spheniscidae*) are found in the world?

(a) 17 or 18 (b) 20 (c) 24 (d) 30

425. Which penguin is distributed throughout the range of the Benguela current?

(a) Peruvian Penguin (*Spheniscus humboldti*)
(b) Jackass Penguin (*Spheniscus demersus*)
(c) Galapagos Penguin (*Spheniscus mendiculus*)
(d) Adelie Penguin (*Pygoscelis adeliae*)

426. Which penguin follows the Humboldt current?

(a) Peruvian Penguin (*Spheniscus humboldti*)
(b) Jackass Penguin (*Spheniscus demersus*)
(c) Galapagos Penguin (*Spheniscus mendiculus*)
(d) Adelie Penguin (*Pygoscelis adeliae*)

427. Which group of aerial birds share the locational range with penguins throughout the world?

(a) Kiwis (*Apterygidae*) (b) Elephant birds (*Aepyornithidae*) (c) Albatrosses (*Diomedeidae*) (d) Shearwaters (*Procellariidae*)

428. Off all the species of penguins which one is the most numerous?

(a) Little Blue Penguin (*Eudyptula minor*)
(b) Adelie Penguin (*Pygoscelis adeliae*)
(c) Emperor Penguin (*Aptenodytes forsteri*)
(d) Peruvian Penguin (*Spheniscus humboldti*)

429. Which is the largest penguin?

(a) Little Blue Penguin (*Eudyptula minor*)
(b) Adelie Penguin (*Pygoscelis adeliae*)
(c) Emperor Penguin (*Aptenodytes forsteri*)
(d) Peruvian Penguin (*Spheniscus humboldti*)

430. Which is the smallest penguin?

(a) Little Blue Penguin (*Eudyptula minor*)
(b) Adelie Penguin (*Pygoscelis adeliae*)
(c) Emperor Penguin (*Aptenodytes forsteri*)
(d) Peruvian Penguin (*Spheniscus humboldti*)

431. Which penguin does not need to come to land as it breeds on the frozen seas of the Antarctica?

(a) Yellow-eyed Penguin (*Megadyptes antipodes*)
(b) King Penguin (*Aptenodyfes patagonica*)
(c) Emperor Penguin (*Aptenodytes forsteri*)
(d) Little Blue Penguin (*Eudyptula minor*)

432. Name the extinct Elephant Bird that laid an egg of two-gallon capacity making it the largest single cell known to science:

(a) *Aepyornis titan* (b) *Apteryx australis* (c) *Apteryx haasti* (d) *Archaeoptenyx lithographica*

433. Name the grebe that was once hunted for its plumes but now protection has ensured its survival in Britain:

(a) Great Crested Grebe (*Podiceps cristatus*) (b) Little Grebe (*Podiceps ruficollis*) (c) Honed Grebe (*Podiceps auritus*) (d) Piedbilled Grebe (*Podilymbus podiceps*)

434. Which bird is the emblem of the naturalists of Bristol?

(a) Taczanowsky's Silver Grebe (*Podiceps taczanowski*) (b) Short-winged Grebe (*Centropelma micropterum*) (c) Piedbilled Grebe (*Podilymbus podiceps*) (d) Pond Heron (*Ardeola grayii*)

435. Name the bird known to have the longest wing span:

(a) Short-tailed Albatross (*Diomedea albatrus*)
(b) Wandering Albatross (*Diomendea exulans*)
(c) Waved Albatross (*Diomedea irrorata*)
(d) Not known

436. Name the albatross endemic to the Hood Island in the Galapagos:

(a) Short-tailed Albatross (*Diomedea albatrus*)
(b) Wandering Albatross (*Diomendea exulans*)
(c) Waved Albatross (*Diomedea irrorata*)
(d) Not known

437. Under what condition would the albatrosses (*Diomedeidae*) be in danger of extinction?

(a) Fishing (b) Economic exploitation of the Southern Hemisphere range for minerals (c) Shooting (d) All the above

438. Which group of birds have a tubed nose?

(a) Storm Petral (*Hydrobatidae*) (b) Albatross (*Diomedeidae*) (c) Shearwaters (*Procellariidae*) (d) Boobies (*Sulidae*)

439. Which bird is known as 'whale bird' because of its adaptation to feeding on plankton in the manner of whales?

(a) Broadbilled Prion (*Pachyptila vittata*)
(b) Reunion Petral (*Petrodroma aterrima*)
(c) Magenta Petral (*Petrodroma magentae*)
(d) Waved Albatross (*Diomedea irrorata*)

440. Name the petral known to science by four specimens only:

(a) Broadbilled Prion (*Pachyptila vittata*)
(b) Reunion Petral (*Petrodroma aterrima*)
(c) Magenta Petral (*Petrodroma magentae*)

441. Name the petral that was collected in 1867 and about which nothing is known since then:

(a) Broadbilled Prion (*Pachyptila vittata*)
(b) Reunion Petral (*Petrodroma aterrima*)
(c) Magenta Petral (*Petrodroma magentae*)

442. Which group of birds is known as 'Mother Carey's chickens'?

(a) Storm Petral (*Hydrobatidae*) (b) Albatross (*Diomedeidae*) (c) Shearwaters (*Procellariidae*) (d) Boobies (*Sulidae*)

443. Which group of birds in the southern hemisphere show remarkable resemblance to the little auk of the Arctic waters?

(a) Diving Petrals (*Pelecanoididae*) (b) Pelicans (*Pelecanidae*) (c) Boobies (*Sulidae*) (d) Herons (*Ardeidae*)

444. Name the only pelican that dives from the air to catch its prey:

(a) Grey Pelican (*Pelecanus philippensis*)
(b) Dalmation Pelican (*Pelecanus crispus*)
(c) Brown Pelican (*Pelecanus occidentalis*)

445. Name the smallest pelican in the world:
   (a) Grey Pelican (*Pelecanus philippensis*)
   (b) Dalmation Pelican (*Pelecanus crispus*)
   (c) Brown Pelican (*Pelecanus occidentalis*)

446. What kind of nest do pelicans (*Pelecanidae*) construct?
   (a) Stick nest on tree tops (b) Mud nest
   (c) Grass nest (d) Cavity nest

447. What is the peculiarity of the flightless cormorant (*Nannopterum harrisi*)?
   (a) It has no natural predators in Galapagos
   (b) Only cormorant that cannot fly (c) All the above

448. Which cormorant of the North Pacific is now extinct due to exploitation for meat?
   (a) Guanay Cormorant (*Phalacrocorax bougainvillii*) (b) Spectacled Cormorant (*Phalacrocorax perspicillatus*) (c) Shag (*Phalacrocorax aristotelis*) (d) Little Cormorant (*Phalacrocorax niger*)

449. What is the typical habitat for Darters (*Anhingidae*)?
   (a) Wooded swamps and mangroves
   (b) Deserts (c) Moist forests (d) Deciduous forests

450. In Florida Everglades and Lake Naivasha in Kenya many species of herons (*Ardeidae*) exist in the same habitat. What is the method of ecological isolation among these birds?
   (a) Distinctive feeding habit (b) Different prey (c) All above (d) None of the above

451. Name a bird found in Mexico, Brazil and Peru that is included in the heron group

(*Ardeidae*) but shows many differences from the group:

(a) Least Bittern (*Ixobrychus exilis*) (b) Agami (*Agami agami*) (c) Japanese Night Heron (*Gorsachius goisagi*) (d) Chinese Egret (*Egretta eulophotus*)

452. Name a bird often called 'white-headed stork', inhabiting the papyrus marshes of the upper Nile:

    (a) White Stork (*Ciconia ciconia*) (b) Shoebill (*Balaeniceps rex*) (c) Hammerhead (*Scopus umbretta*) (d) Adjutant (*Leptoptilos dubius*)

453. Name the legendary bird associated with the myth in Europe that it brings human babies:

    (a) White Stork (*Ciconia ciconia*) (b) Shoebill (*Balaenceps rex*) (c) Hammerhead (*Scopus umbretta*) (d) Adjutant (*Leptoptilos dubius*)

454. What is the food habit of the African marabou stork (*Leptoptilos crumeniferus*), the adjutant (*Leptoptilos dubius*) and the lesses adjutant (*Leptoptilos javanicus*)?

    (a) Herbivore (b) Carnivore (c) Omnivore (d) Scavenger

455. As an adaptation, the African openbilled stork (*Anastomus lamelligerus*) and the Asiatic openbilled stork (*Anastomus oscitans*) have a gap between the mandibles which meet only at the tip and the base. What is the main food item of these birds?

    (a) Snakes (b) Leaves (c) Fish (d) Snails

456. Name the only stork found in the U.S.A.:

    (a) Saddlebilled Stork (*Ephippiorhynchus senegalensis*) (b) Jabiru (*Jabiru mycteria*)

71

(c) Wood Stork (*Mycteria americana*) (d) White Stork (*Ciconia ciconia*)

457. Name the bird that was revered and mummified by the ancient Egyptians:

(a) Japanese Crested Ibis (*Niponia nippon*)
(b) Scarlet Ibis (*Guara ruber*) (c) Sacred Ibis (*Threskiornis aethiopica*) (d) Jabiru (*Jabiru mycteria*)

458. Which bird is the emblem of the British Ornithologists' Union?

(a) Japanese Crested Ibis (*Nipponia nippon*)
(b) Scarlet Ibis (*Guara ruber*) (c) Sacred Ibis (*Threskiornis aethiopica*) (d) Jabiru (*Jabiru mycteria*)

459. Which bird was considered to be a reincarnation of the Egyptian god *Iboth* and was represented as an 'Ibis-headed man'?

(a) Japanese Crested Ibis (*Nipponia nippon*)
(b) Scarlet Ibis (*Guara ruber*) (c) Sacred Ibis (*Threskiornis aethiopica*) (d) Jabiru (*Jabiru mycteria*)

460. Which stork is now extinct in Egypt and found only in Africa, south of Sahara and the Persian Gulf?

(a) Japanese Crested Ibis (*Nipponia nippon*)
(b) Scarlet Ibis (*Guara ruber*) (c) Sacred Ibis (*Threskiornis aethiopica*) (d) Jabiru (*Jabiru mycteria*)

461. Which is considered the most beautiful ibis in the world?

(a) Japanese Crested Ibis (*Nipponia nippon*)
(b) Scarlet Ibis (*Guara ruber*) (c) Sacred Ibis (*Threskiornis aethiopica*) (d) Jabiru (*Jabiru mycteria*)

462. Which is the largest and most widespread species of flamingo?

(a) Greater Flamingo (*Phoenicopterus ruber*)
(b) Andean Flamingo (*Phoenicoparrus andinus*)
(c) James Flamingo (*P. jamesi*) (d) Lesser Flamingo (*Phoeniconaias minor*)

463. Which group of birds lack the strengthening of the rib cage found in all other birds except the fossil *Archaeopteryx lithographica*?

(a) Ducks (*Anatidae*) (b) Screamers (*Anhimidae*)
(c) Megapodes (*Megapodiidae*) (d) Storm Petral (*Hydrobatidae*)

464. Down feathers are harvested from the lining of nests of many ducks for commercial use. Which bird supposedly provides the warmest down feathers?

(a) Crested Shelduck (*Tadorna cristata*)
(b) Eurasian Shelduck (*Tadorna todarna*)
(c) Eider (*Somateria mollissima*) (d) Goosander (*Mergus merganser*)

465. Which of the following species of duck is extinct?

(a) Goosander (*Mergus merganser*)
(b) Pinkheaded Duck (*Rhodonessa caryophyllacea*) (c) Shovelbilled Pink-eared Duck (*Malacorhynchus membranaceus*) (d) Nene (*Branta sandvicensis*)

466. Which bird is the ancestor of domestic geese?

(a) Barheaded Goose (*Anser indicus*) (b) Greyleg Goose (*Anser anser*) (c) Swan Goose (*Anser cygnoides*) (d) Nene Goose (*Branta sandvicensis*)

467. A species of goose in Hawaii which was under threat of extinction due to over-exploitation, and from predators introduced by man, has

survived by being bred in captivity at Slimbridge and a return to the wild. Name it:

(a) Nene Goose (*Branta sandvicensis*)
(b) Canada Goose (*B. canadensis*) (c) Barnacle Goose (*B. leucopsis*) (d) Swan Goose (*Anser cygnoides*)

468. Name a predator vulture of the Guano Islands:

(a) California Condor (*Gymnogyps californianus*)
(b) Turkey Vulture (*Cathartes aura*) (c) Black Vulture (*Coragyps atratus*) (d) Cape Vulture (*Gyps coprotheres*)

469. Name the vulture under threat of being shot out of existence:

(a) California Condor (*Gymnogyps californianus*)
(b) Turkey Vulture (*Cathartes aura*) (c) Black Vulture (*Coragyps atratus*) (d) Cape Vulture (*Gyps coprotheres*)

470. Name a vulture that feeds on oil-palm fruits, though its diet includes the dead fish also:

(a) Turkey Vulture (*Cathartus aura*)
(b) Hooded Vulture (*Necrosytes monachus*)
(c) Lammerglier (*Gypaetus barbatus*)
(d) Palmnut Vulture (*Gypohierax angolensis*)

471. What is the difference between eagles and buzzards in flight?

(a) Eagles have short tail and prominent head
(b) Buzzards have shorter tail and very small head (c) All above

472. Which bird is the national symbol of the U.S.A.?

(a) Bald Eagle (*Haliaeetus leucocephalus*)
(b) Golden Eagle (*Aquila chrysaetos*) (c) Tawny

Eagle (*Aquila rapax*) (d) Palmnut Vulture (*Gypohierax angolensis*)

473. Which bird of prey feeds exclusively on fish?

(a) Imperial Eagle (*Aquila heliaca*) (b) Osprey (*Pandion haliaetus*) (c) African Fish Eagle (*Haliaeetus yocifer*) (d) Crowned Eagle (*Harpyhaliaetus coronatus*)

474. What is the food of the Everglade Kite (*Rostrhamus sociabilis*) and Hookbilled Kite (*Chondrohierax uncinatus*)?

(a) Snakes (b) Fish (c) Grains (d) Snails

475. Name the smallest bird of prey in the world:

(a) African Pygmy Falcon (*Poliohyierax semitorguatus*) (b) Philippine Falconet (*Microhierax erythrogonys*) (c) Gyrfalcon (*Falco rusticolus*) (d) Grey Falcon (*Falco hypoleucos*)

476. In which country did the art of faclonry originate?

(a) U.S.S.R. (b) India (c) U.S.A. (d) China

477. What is the source of heat for incubation of eggs of the megapodes (*Megapodiidae*)?

(a) Heat of the sun and heat generated by decay of vegetation (b) Body heat (c) Geothermic heat

478. How many species of grouse (*Tetraonidae*) are found in the world?

(a) 10 (b) 12 (c) 15 (d) 17

479. Which feathers are used by the peafowl (*Pavo cristatus*) for its display?

(a) Tail feathers (b) Elongated feathers of upper tail coverts (c) Down feathers (d) Wing feathers

480. Which bird is the ancestor of the chicken?

(a) Red Junglefowl (*Gallus gallus*) (b) Blood Pheasant (*Ithaginus cruentus*) (c) Peofowl (*Pavo cristatus*) (d) Common Turkey (*Meleagris gallopavo*)

481. Which turkey is the most domesticated of the two species?

(a) Common Turkey (*Meleagris gallopavo*)
(b) Ocellated Turkey (*Agriocharis ocellata*)

482. Identify the bird with the short and decurved bill in which the upper mandible is not fused with the skull, and which has red eyes and eyelashes like mammals:

(a) Whooping Crane (*Grus americana*)
(b) Hoatzin (*Opisthocomus hoazin*) (c) Common Turkey (*Meleagris gallopavo*) (d) Common Crane (*Grus grus*)

483. Where are the mesites (*Mesitornithidae*) found?

(a) China (b) Madagascar (c) Japan (d) India

484. Name the rarest crane in the world:

(a) Whooping Crane (*Grus americana*)
(b) Japanese Crane (*Grus Japonensia*)
(c) Sandhill Crane (*Grus canadensis*)
(d) Crowned Crane (*Balearica pavonina*)

485. How many genera of cranes (*Gruidae*) are found in the world?

(a) 1 (b) 2 (c) 3 (d) 4

486. Name the crane which has flaps of skin on the sides of its face:

(a) Wattled Crane (*Bugeranus carunculatus*)
(b) Stanley Crane (*Anthropoides paradisea*)
(c) Crowned Crane (*Balearica pavonina*)
(d) Common Crane (*Grus grus*)

487. Which is the tallest crane in the world?

(a) Common Crane (*Grus grus*) (b) Hooded Crane (*Grus monacha*) (c) Sarus Crane (*Grus antigone*) (d) Whitenaped Crane (*Grus vipio*)

488. Which is the world's tallest flying bird?

(a) Common Crane (*Grus grus*) (b) Hooded Crane (*Grus monacha*) (c) Sarus Crane (*Grus antigone*) (d) Whitenaped Crane (*Grus vipio*)

489. Which bird was the symbol of Roman power?

(a) Solitaire (*Raphus solitarius*) (b) Golden Eagle (*Aquila chrysaeetos*) (c) Osprey (*Pandion haliatus*) (d) Sarus Crane (*Grus antigone*)

490. What is the distribution of the penguins in the world?

(a) Only in the southern hemisphere (b) Only in the northern hemisphere (c) Near the temperate regions (d) All over the world

491. The giant moa (*Dinornis maximus*) is an extinct bird. Where was it found when living?

(a) Nepal (b) New Zealand (c) India (d) Algeria

492. What was the main reason for the extinction of the huia (*Heteralocha acutirostris*), a bird of New Zealand which was last sighted in the year 1907?

(a) Feather trade (b) Natural predation (c) Racial senescence (d) Killing for food

493. Its habit of returning to try and help wounded flockmates made it vulnerable before the hunter. Thus did this north American parrot become extinct. Name it:

(a) Beautiful Parakeet (*Psephotus pulcherrimus*)
(b) Carolina Parakeet (*Conuropsis carolinesis*)

(c) Splendid Parakeet (*Neophema splendida*)

(d) Vulturina Parrot (*Psittrichas fulgidus*)

494. Name the only group of birds in which nostrils open at the tip of the bill:

(a) Ducks (b) Parrots (c) Owls (d) Kiwis

495. Where are kiwis found?

(a) New Zealand (b) South America (c) Australia (d) Italy

496. Where is the ostrich (*Struthio camelus*) found in the wild?

(a) India (b) South America (c) Yugoslavia (d) Africa

497. Where is the rhea (*Rhea americana*) found?

(a) Brazil (b) India (c) Australia (d) South America

498. How many species of birds in the world are known only from the fossils?

(a) 600 (b) 700 (c) 800 (d) 900

499. How many species of birds have fossil as well as living representatives today?

(a) 500 (b) 600 (c) 700 (d) 800

500. The Massa National Park provides the breeding site for nearly half of the world's population of the waldrap ibis (*Geronticus eremita*). Where is it located?

(a) Bolivia (b) Siberia (c) Morocco (d) Canada

501. Which country has the maximum number of species of cranes in the world?

(a) China (b) India (c) South Africa (d) USSR

502. Which African bird is popularly known as 'snake-killer'?

(a) Goshawk (*Accipiter gentilis*) (b) Secretary Bird (*Sagittarius serpentarius*) (c) Osprey (*Pandion haliaetus*) (d) Rhea (*Rhea americana*)

503. Name the largest flying bird (now fossil) that ever lived on earth:

(a) *Columba leuconota* (b) *Ducula badia* (c) *Teratornis incredibilis* (d) *Heteralocha acutirostris*

504. Which bird is exploited by Venezuelans to obtain cooking oil?

(a) Redbilled Quelea (*Quelea quelea*) (b) Oil Bird (*Steatornis caripensis*) (c) Passenger Pigeon (*Ectopistes migratorius*) (d) Limpkin (*Aramus quarauna*)

505. Name the most crop destructive bird in the world:

(a) Redbilled Quelea (*Quelea quelea*) (b) Oil Bird (*Steatornis caripensis*) (c) Passenger Pigeon (*Ectopistes migratorius*) (d) Limpkin (*Aramus quarauna*)

506. Which one of the following birds is extinct?

(a) Redbilled Quelea (*Quelea quelea*) (b) Oil Bird (*Steatornis caripensis*) (c) Passenger Pigeon (*Ectopistes migratorius*) (d) Limpkin (*Aramus quarauna*)

507. Which is the only bird in the world having a bill laterally bent to the right?

(a) Limpkin (*Aramus quarauna*) (b) Golden Plover (*Pluvialis dominica*) (c) Wrybill (*Anarhynchus frontalis*) (d) Oil Bird (*Steatornis caripensis*)

508. Which bird forms the connecting link between the cranes and the rails?

(a) Limpkin (*Aramus quarauna*) (b) Golden Plover (*Pluvialis dominica*) (c) Wrybill (*Anarhynchus frontalis*) (d) Oil Bird (*Steatornis caripensis*)

509. What was the cause for the decline of the crane population in the world?

(a) Draining of wetlands (b) Persistent hunting (c) All the above (d) A plague which decimated their numbers

510. Which crane is being used as a foster parent for hatching eggs of the whooping crane (*Grus americana*) at Wood Buffalo National Park, Canada, to establish a second population at Idaho?

(a) Sandhill Crane (*Grus canadensis*) (b) Hooded crane (*Grus monacha*) (c) Sarus Crane (*Grus antigone*) (d) Red Crowned Crane (*Grus japonensis*)

511. Which crane is regarded as the traditional Chinese symbol of good fortune?

(a) White-naped crane (*Grus vipio*) (b) Red-crowned Crane (*Grus japonensis*) (c) Crowned Crane (*Grus pavonina*) or (*Balaearica pavonina*) (d) Sandhill Crane (*Grus canadensis*)

512. In which continent is the maximum number of species of coots (*Fulica* sp.) found?

(a) Australia (b) Africa (c) Asia (d) South America

513. Which species of coot uses stones for its nest, contrary to other coots' floating nests made of vegetation?

(a) Purplo Gallinule (*Prophyrio prophyrio*) (b) Takahe (*Notornis mantelli*) (c) Horned Coot (*Fulica cornuta*) (d) Common Coot (*Fulica atra*)

514. A bird which was known only from fossil remains till 1849, and from skin remains till 1898, when it was again declared extinct, was rediscovered in the year 1948 by Dr. G.B. Orbell, and is now protected at Lake Te Anau in Murchison Mountains of New Zealand's South Island. Identify it:

(a) Purplo Gallinule (*Porphyrio prophyrio*) (b) Takahe (*Notornis mantelli*) (c) Horned Coot (*Fulica cornuta*) (d) Common Coot (*Fulica atra*)

515. Name the only place in the world where the kagu (*Rhynochetos jubatus*) is found:

(a) New Caledonia (b) Australia (c) Andaman (d) Lake Te Anau

516. What is the reason for the decline in the population of the Great Bustard (*Otis tarda*)?

(a) Persecution of bird and eggs (b) Ploughing of open plain for cultivation (c) All above (d) None of the above

517. Name the rarest bustard in the world?

(a) Great Indian Bustard (*Choriotis nigriceps*) (b) Arabian Bustard (*Andeotis arabs*) (c) Kori Bustard (*Ardeotis kori*) (d) Great Bustard (*Otis trada*)

518. Which bird is utilized as a mobile perch by the carmine bee eaters (*Merops nubicus*)?

(a) Great Indian Bustard (*Choriotis nigriceps*) (b) Kori Bustard (*Ardeotis kori*) (c) Arabian Bustard (*Andeotis arabs*) (d) Great Bustard (*Otis trada*)

519. How many species of jacanas (*Jacanidae*) are found in the world?

(a) 4 (b) 5 (c) 6 (d) 7

520. How many genera of jacana are found in the world?

(a) 3 (b) 4 (c) 5 (d) 7

521. Which group of birds is called 'lily-trotters'?

(a) Jacana (*Jacanidae*) (b) Plovers (*Charadriidae*) (c) Crab-plover (*Dromadidae*) (d) Pittas (*Pittidae*)

522. Which species of jacana cannot fly?

(a) African Jacana (*Actophilornis africana*) (b) Madagascar Jacana (*A. albinucha*) (c) All the above (d) Bronzed-winged Jacana (*Metopidius indicus*)

523. Name the only group of birds that has precocial chicks:

(a) Jacana (*Jacanidae*) (b) Painted Snipe (*Rostratulidae*) (c) Both the above (d) None of the above

524. Which species of the jacana female lays up to ten eggs in the nests of different males which incubate them?

(a) Pheasant-tailed Jacana (*Hydrophasianus chirurgus*) (b) Bronze-winged Jacana (*Metopidius indicus*) (c) Australian Jacana (*Irediparra gallinacea*) (d) African Jacana (*Actophilornis africana*)

525. Which bird is known as the 'lotus bird'?

(a) Pheasant-tailed Jacana (*Hydrophasianus chirurgus*) (b) Bronze-winged Jacana (*Metopidius indicus*) (c) Australian Jacana (*Irediparra gallinacea*) (d) African Jacana (*Actophilornis africana*)

526. How many species of plover (*Charadriidae*) are found in the world?

(a) 26 (b) 36 (c) 46 (d) 56

527. Which American bird produces 'kill-dee' calls?

(a) Golden Plover (*Pluvialis apricaria*)
(b) Killdeer (*Charadrius haiticula*) (c) Lapwing
(*Vanellus vanellus*) (d) Wrybill (*Anarhynchus frondalis*)

528. Which European bird produces 'pee-wee' calls?

(a) Golden Plover (*Pluvialis apricaria*)
(b) Killdeer (*Charadrius haiticula*) (c) Lapwing
(*Vanellus vanellus*) (d) Wrybill (*Anarhynchus frondalis*)

529. Which of the following birds was exploited to the extent of feared extinction in Labrador?

(a) Eskimo Curlew (*Numenius borealis*) (b) Ruff
(*Philomachus pugnax*) (c) Dunlin (*Calidris alpina*)
(d) Golden Plover (*Pluvialis apricaria*)

530. Which sandpiper has the spatulate bill?

(a) Redshank (*Tringa totanus*) (b) Spoonbilled
Sandpiper (*Eurynorhynchus pygmeus*) (c) Least
Sandpiper (*Calidris minutilla*) (d) Cox's
Sandpiper (*Calidris paramelanotus*)

531. Name the only bird of the thick-knees family (*Burhinidae*) that is migratory and forms flocks:

(a) Stone Curlew (*Burhinus oedicnemus*)
(b) Water Dikkop (*B. vermiculatus*) (c) Inca
Tern (*Larosterna inca*) (d) Eskimo Curlew
(*Nemenius borealis*)

532. Name the Antarctic bird with unwebbed feet:

(a) Yellow-billed Sheatbill (*Chionis alba*)
(b) Black-billed Sheatbill (*C. minor*) (c) Both
above (d) Not known

533. Name the only tern (*Laridae*) that breeds in burrows and cavities:

(a) Inca Tern (*Larosterna inca*) (b) Arctic Tern (*Sterna paradisaea*) (c) Caspian Tern (*Hydroprogne caspia*) (d) Black Tern (*Chlidonias niger*)

534. Which bird covers the maximum distance during migration?

(a) Inca Tern (*Larosterna inca*) (b) Arctic Tern (*Sterna paradisaea*) (c) Caspian Tern (*Hydroprogne caspia*) (d) Black Tern (*Chlidonias niger*)

535. Which is the only group of birds that has a longer lower mandible than the upper one?

(a) Sandgrouse (*Pteroclididae*) (b) Auks (*Alcidae*) (c) Skimmers (*Rynchopidae*) (d) Terns (*Laridae*)

536. Which group of birds is the northern counterpart of the penguins of the southern hemisphere?

(a) Sandgrouse (*Pteroclididae*) (b) Auks (*Alcidae*) (c) Skimmers (*Rynchopidae*) (d) Terns (*Laridae*)

537. All the living auks are capable of flying but the extinct species was flightless. Name it:

(a) Great Auk (*Pinguinus impennis*) (b) Little Auk (*Plautus alle*) (c) Crested Auklet (*Aethia cristatella*) (d) All the above

538. What is the main cause for the decline in the population of the seabirds?

(a) Oil pollution of seas (b) Shooting and egg collection (c) All above (d) None of the above

539. Which species of the dove shows sexual dimorphism and has a remarkably long tail?
(a) Namaqua Dove (*Oena capensis*) (b) Rock Dove (*Columba livia*) (c) Heart Pigeon (*Gallicolumba*) (d) Ring Dove (*Streptopelia decaocta*)

540. Passenger pigeons (*Ectopistes migratorius*) numbered in the millions in North America and were hunted out of existence. When and where did the last specimen die?
(a) Cincinnati Zoo, 1914 (b) National Zoological Park, Delhi, 1956 (c) Sanjay Biological Park, Patna, 1970 (d) Udaipur Zoo, 1991

541. Name a scavenger parrot found in New Zealand:
(a) Kea (*Nestor notabilis*) (b) Australian Ground Parrot (*Pezoporus wallicus*) (c) African Grey Parrot (*Psittacus erithacus*) (d) Monk Parakeet (*Myiopsitta monachus*)

542. Name a flightless parrot that nests on the ground unlike its cavity-nesting counterparts:
(a) Kea (*Nestor notabilis*) (b) Australian Ground Parrot (*Pezoporus wallicus*) (c) African Grey Parrot (*Psittacus erithacus*) (d) Monk Parakeet (*Myiopsitta monachus*)

543. Which is the smallest parrot in the world?
(a) Kea (*Nestor notabilis*) (b) Orange-fronted Hanging Parrot (*Loriculus aurantiifrons*) (c) Kakapo (*Strigops habroptilus*) (d) Monk Parakeet (*Myiopsitta monachus*)

544. Of the 45 species of cuckoo in the world, how many show brood parasitism?
(a) 10 (b) 41 (c) 43 (d) All 45

545. Which cuckoo has adapted the gliding movement, as its small, rounded wings are unable to generate sustained flight?

(a) Squirrel Cuckoo (*Piaya cayana*) (b) Banded Ground Cuckoo (*Neomorphus radiolosus*) (c) Sunda Ground Cuckoo (*Carpococcyx radiceus*) (d) Cocos Cuckoo (*Coccyzus ferrugineus*)

546. What is the distribution range of the snowy owl (*Nyctea scandiaca*)?

(a) Northern tundra (b) Equator (c) Andes (d) India

547. What is the nesting site selected by the elf owl (*Micrathene whitneyi*) of North America?

(a) Rock crevices (b) Cavities in cacti (c) Cavities in trees (d) Treetops

548. How many species of eagle owls are found in the world?

(a) 9 (b) 10 (c) 11 (d) 12

549. To which genus do all the 12 species of eagle owls belong?

(a) *Surnia* (b) *Tyto* (c) *Bubo* (d) *Athene*

550. How many species of barn owls are there?

(a) 6 (b) 8 (c) 9 (d) 10

551. Which is the largest owl in the world?

(a) Spotted Eagle Owl (*Bubo capensis*) (b) Milky Eagle Owl (*Bubo lacteus*) (c) Eurasian Eagle Owl (*Bubo bubo*) (d) Bay Owl (*Phodilus badius*)

552. What is the nest site selected by the eagle owls (*Bubo* sp.)?

(a) Unlined depression on the ground (b) Treetop (c) Ground burrow (d) Tree cavity

553. Though owls are primarily woodland birds, one species has taken to the ground and developed long legs for excavating the ground, roost and fast running to adapt itself to American prairies. Name it:

(a) Pel's Fishing Owl (*Scottopelia peli*) (b) Burrowing Owl (*Speotyto cunicularia*) (c) Spectacled Owl (*Pulsatrix perspicillata*) (d) Barn Owl (*Tyto alba*)

554. To maintain the owl population in a woodland, what managment strategy should be followed?

(a) Retention of the potential cavity roost trees (b) Fire protection and snag retention (c) Both the above (d) No specific management

555. If dead, dying and diseased trees from a woodland are removed in order to manage the forests of the tropics for timber, what effect will this have on the population of the owls?

(a) Increase in population (b) Decrease in population (c) No effect on the population

556. The nocturnal oilbird (*Steatornis caripensis*) from which native Venezuelans obtain cooking oil, lives in deep caves. How does it navigate in the pitch darkness?

(a) By sight (b) By echolocation (c) By thermal waves (d) By magnetism

557. What is the food habit of the guacharo or oilbird (*Steatornis caripensis*)?

(a) Caprophagous (b) Insectivorous
(c) Frugivorous (d) Omnivorous

558. Name the birds related to the nightjars
(*Caprimulgidae*) but are, however, arboreal,
unlike the ground dwelling nightjars:

(a) Frogmouths (*Podargidae*) (b) Mousebirds
(*Coliidae*) (c) Trogons (*Trogonidae*) (d) Owls
(*Strigidae*)

559. In the different bird families of the order
Caprimulgiformes techniques to catch prey vary.
Nightjars obtain food by hawking in the air,
frogmouths by pouncing like a shrike and
potoos as flycatchers. What technique is used
by the owlet-frogmouths?

(a) Ground feeding (b) Pouncing (c) Hawking (d) Flycatching

560. Which North American swift has adapted
factory chimneys as nesting sites?

(a) Eurasian Swift (*Apus apus*) (b) Chimney
Swift (*Chaetura pelagica*) (c) Palm Swift (*Cypsiurus parvus*) (d) Fernando Po Swift (*Apus
sladeniae*)

561. Name the bird which makes nests by gluing
feathers to the underside of a palm leaf and
sticks eggs to the nest. On hatching, the chicks
must immediately cling to the nest until
fledged:

(a) Black-nest Swiftlet (*Aerodramus maximus*)
(b) White-nest Swiftlet (*Aerodramus fuciphagus*)
(c) Palm Swift (*Cypsiurus parvus*) (d) Giant
Swiftlet (*Apus acuticauda*)

562. How many species of the hummingbird
(*Trochilidae*) are to be found in the world?

(a) 120 (b) 220 (c) 310 (d) 320

563. Name the world's smallest bird that weighs less than 2 grams and measures a little over 2 inches:

(a) Cuban Bee Hummingbird (*Mellisuga helenae*) (b) Andean Giant Hummingbird (*Patagona gigas*) (c) Ruby-throated Hummingbird (*Archilochus colubris*) (d) Rufous Hummingbird (*Selasphorus rufus*)

564. Which hummingbird, despite its less than 9 cm size, performs the extraordinary migratory journey across the Gulf of Mexico and West Indies to South America covering a distance of over 800 km?

(a) Cuban Bee Hummingbird (*Mellisuga helenae*) (b) Andean Giant Hummingbird (*Patagona gigas*) (c) Ruby-throated Hummingbird (*Archilochus colubris*) (d) Rufous Hummingbird (*Selasphorus rufus*)

565. Which is the largest hummingbird in the world?

(a) Cuban Bee Hummingbird (*Mellisuga helenae*) (b) Andean Giant Hummingbird (*Patagona gigas*) (c) Ruby-throated Hummingbird (*Archilochus colubris*) (d) Rufous Hummingbird (*Selasphorus rufus*)

566. Which bird has, in proportion to its body size, the longest bill of all birds in the world?

(a) Sword-billed Hummingbird (*Ensifera ensifera*) (b) Rufous Hummingbird (*Selasphorus rufus*) (c) Ruby-throated Hummingbird (*Archilochus colubris*) (d) Andean Giant Hummingbird (*Patagona giagas*)

567. Name the only species of hummingbird that nests in eastern U.S.A. and Canada:

(a) Sword-billed Hummingbird (*Ensifera ensifera*) (b) Rufous Hummingbird (*Selasphorus rufus*) (c) Ruby-throated Hummingbird (*Archilochus colubris*) (d) Andean Giant Hummingbird (*Patagona giagas*)

568. Name the hummingbird found furthest north that breeds as far north as southern Alaska:

(a) Sword-billed Hummingbird (*Ensifera ensifera*) (b) Rufous Hummingbird (*Selasphorus rufus*) (c) Ruby-throated Hummingbird (*Archilochus colubris*) (d) Andean Giant Hummingbird (*Patagona giagas*)

569. Which group of birds was captured in millions, for their brilliant coloured tough skins, during the nineteenth century, to adorn women's hats in Europe?

(a) Todies (*Todidae*) (b) Hummingbirds (*Trochilidae*) (c) Motmots (*Momotidae*) (d) Trogons (*Trogonidae*)

570. How many species of trogons (*Trogonidae*) are to be found in the world?

(a) 5 (b) 15 (c) 25 (d) 35

571. What is the nest site of the trogons (*Trogonidae*)?

(a) Cavity on decaying wood (b) Treetops (c) Floating vegetation (d) Ground

572. Name the national bird of Guatemala:

(a) Resplendent Quetzal (*Pharomachrus mocino*) (b) Gartered Trogon (*Chrysotrogon caligatus*) (c) Great Jacamar (*Jacamerops aurea*) (d) Little Kingfisher (*Alcyone pusilla*)

573. Name the smallest kingfisher (*Alcedinidae*) in the world:

(a) Laughing Kookaburra (*Dacelo novaeguinae*)
(b) Little Kingfisher (*Alcyone pusilla*) (c) Hook-billed Kingfisher (*Melidora macrorrhina*)
(d) Pied Kingfisher (*Ceryle rudis*)

574. Which kingfisher excavates a nest in the nests of tree-termites?

(a) Laughing Kookaburra (*Dacelo novaeguinae*)
(b) Little Kingfisher (*Alcyone pusilla*) (c) Hook-billed Kingfisher (*Melidora macrorrhina*)
(d) Pied Kingfisher (*Ceryle rudis*)

575. How many species of hornbill (*Bucerotidae*) are to be found in the world?

(a) 15 (b) 25 (c) 35 (d) 45

576. Name the hornbill species that congregates in large flocks during lunch time to feed on bits at Kilaguni Lodge of the Tsavo National Park:

(a) Red-billed Hornbill (*Tockus camurus*)
(b) Great Hornbill (*Buceros bicornis*)
(c) Rhinoceros Hornbill (*Buceros rhinoceros*)
(d) Wreathed Hornbill (*Rhyticeros undulatus*)

577. Which is the largest of all tree-dwelling hornbills in the world?

(a) Red-billed Hornbill (*Tockus camurus*)
(b) Great Hornbill (*Buceros bicornis*)
(c) Rhinoceros Hornbill (*Buceros rhinoceros*)
(d) Wreathed Hornbill (*Rhyticeros undulatus*)

578. How many species of barbets (*Capitonidae*) are to be found in the world?

(a) 46 (b) 56 (c) 66 (d) 76

579. What is the nesting habit of the barbets (*Capitonidae*)?

(a) Hole-nesting (b) Ground-nesting
(c) Water-nesting (d) None of the above

580. Name the bird that feeds on honey-comb wax:

(a) Greater Honeyguide (*Indicator indicator*)
(b) Coppersmith (*Megalaima haemacephala*)
(c) D'Arnaud's Barbet (*Trachyphonus darnaudii*)
(d) Crimson-hooded Honeyeater (*Myzomela kuehni*)

581. Which bird leads men and some animals to the honeybee combs and when the honey has been extracted, feeds on the wax?

(a) Greater Honeyguide (*Indicator indicator*)
(b) Coppersmith (*Megalaima haemacephala*)
(c) D'Arnaud's Barbet (*Trachyphonus darnaudii*)
(d) Crested Honeycreeper (*Palmeria dolei*)

582. What is the reason for the decline in population of the ivory-billed woodpecker (*Campephilus principalis*) in southern U.S.A.?

(a) Non-availability of large cavity nest trees and old stands (b) Shooting (c) Both above (d) Not known

583. Pittas (*Pittidae*) are concentrated in southeast Asia where more than half of the total number of the species are found. What is the total number of species of pittas?

(a) 5 (b) 15 (c) 19 (d) 23

584. Name a bird of New Zealand which nobody has seen alive except a light-house keeper, for it was eaten away to extinction in 1894 by a cat owned by him:

(a) New Zealand Bush Wren (*Xenicus longipes*)
(b) Rifleman (*Acanthisitta chloris*) (c) Stephen

Island Rock Wren (*Xenicus lyalli*) (d) Superb Lyrebird (*Menura superba*)

585. Which bird is the national emblem of Australia?

(a) Superb Lyrebird (*Menura superba*) (b) Albert's Lyrebird (*Menura alberti*) (c) Rifleman (*Acanthisitta chloris*) (d) Wood Lark (*Lullua arborea*)

586. Name the only lark found in North America except the introduced skylark (*Alauda arvensis*):

(a) Wood Lark (*Lullula arborea*) (b) Crested Lark (*Galerida cristata*) (c) Shore Lark (*Eremophila alpestris*) (d) Ash's Lark (*Mirafra ashi*)

587. Which is the only lark of South America?

(a) Wood Lark (*Lullula arborea*) (b) Crested Lark (*Galerida cristata*) (c) Shore Lark (*Eremophila alpestris*) (d) Botha's Lark (*Spizocorys fringillaris*)

588. Name the main centre where about two-thirds of the world's species of the lark are found:

(a) Asia (b) Australia (c) North America (d) Africa

589. What is the difference between the swift and the swallow?

(a) Swifts have longer wings (b) Swallows have long forked tail (c) Both the above (d) None of the above

590. All wagtails bob their tails up and down except one which moves it from side to side. Name this species:

(a) White Wagtail (*Motacilla alba*) (b) Yellow Wagtail (*M. flava*) (c) Forest Wagtail (*Dendronanthus indicus*) (d) Grey Wagtail (*Motacilla cinerea*)

591. Which bulbul has been introduced into Australia?

(a) Redvented Bulbul (*Pycnonotus cafer*)
(b) Brown-eared Bulbul (*Hypsipetes amaurotis*)
(c) Redwhiskered Bulbul (*Pycnonotus jacosus*)
(d) Wattled Bulbul (*Pycnonotus nieuwenhuisi*)

592. Which group of birds is called the 'water walker' due to the ability to walk on the bed of a fast flowing stream?

(a) Palmchat (*Dulidae*) (b) Dipper (*Cinclidae*)
(c) Vangas (*Vangidae*) (d) Terns (*Laridae*)

593. Which bird is considered the best song bird?

(a) Nightingale (*Luscinia megarhynchos*) (b) Indian Robin (*Sexicoloides fulicata*) (c) American Robin (*Turdus migratorius*) (d) Freira (*Pterodroma madeira*)

594. A flowerpecker in Australia is called the mistletoe-bird (*Dicaeum hirundinaceum*). Why?

(a) Its food is the berries of mistletoe (b) It spreads this unwanted plant parasite (c) Both above (d) No reason

595. Which group of birds is the Asian counterparts of the North American hummingbirds?

(a) Sunbirds (b) White-eyes (c) Flowerpeckers (d) Warblers

596. What is the food of the sunbirds (*Nectariniidae*)?

(a) Flower nectar (b) Fruits (c) Insects (d) Leaves

597. What is the place of origin of the honeyeaters (*Meliphagidae*)?

(a) Australasia (b) Africa (c) South America (d) Asia

598. Name the most northerly breeding land bird:

(a) Junco (*Junco hyemalis*) (b) Snow Bunting (*Plectrophenax nivalis*) (c) Mistletoe Bird (*Dicaeum hirundinaceum*) (d) Redbilled Quelea (*Quelea quelea*)

599. What is the main reason for the extinction of many species of the Hawaiian honeycreeppers (*Drepanididae*)?

(a) Introduction of exotic pest animals (b) Shooting (c) Capture (d) Fire

600. Where are the Darwin's finches to be found?

(a) Galapagos Islands (b) India (c) Sumatra (d) Bali

601. What is a bower?

(a) Courting structure built by male birds to secure a female (b) It is seen in the Bowerbirds only (c) Both above (d) Not known

602. Where are the highest number of species of the birds of paradise found?

(a) India (b) Australia (c) New Guinea (d) Kenya

603. What management strategy is followed in moorlands managed for grouse which feed mostly on young shoots?

(a) Control burning of compartments at different stages (b) Young shoots in recently burnt areas provide food while older areas

provide cover and nest site (c) All above
(d) No specific management

604. What is the reason for the extinction of the elephant birds of Madagascar?

(a) Invasion of the islands by people who could easily shoot these flightless birds (b) Predation by introduced pest (c) Both above (d) Not known

605. Which bird gives its name to the currency of Guatemala?

(a) Quetzal (*Pharomachrus mocino*) (b) Short-eared Owl (*Asio flammeus*) (c) Black Wood-pecker (*Dryocopus maritus*) (d) David's Owl (*Strix davidi*)

606. Which is the largest woodpecker in Europe?

(a) Quetzal (*Pharomachrus mocino*) (b) Short-eared Owl (*Asio flammeus*) (c) Black Wood-pecker (*Dryocopus maritus*) (d) Robust Woodpecker (*Campephilus robustus*)

607. Crossbills have a peculiar bill which enables them to obtain its special food. What is the food?

(a) Seeds from the pine cones (b) Fruits (c) Mollusc (d) Leaves

608. Which is the smallest owl in the world?

(a) Elf Owl (*Micrathene whitneyi*) (b) Pygmy Owl (*Glaucidium minutissimum*) (c) Shorteared Owl (*Asio flammeus*) (d) Barn Owl (*Tyto alba*)

609. Which condor is facing the danger of extinction as there are less than 30 of these surviving in the wild?

(a) Andean Condor (*Vultur gryphus*)
(b) California condor (*Vultur californianus*)
(c) Both above (d) None

610. How many species of pelicans are to be found in the world?

(a) 4 (b) 5 (c) 6 (d) 7

611. Name the world's heaviest living parrot, found in New Zealand, that moves in leaps:

(a) Kakapo (*Strigops habroptilus*) (b) Muller's Parrot (*Tanygnathus sumatranus*) (c) Carolina Parakeet (*Conuropsis carolinensis*) (d) Thick-billed Parrot (*Rhynchopsitta pachyrhyncha*)

612. Many species of island dwelling parrots have become extinct and many are threatened with extinction. What is the reason?

(a) Habitat destruction and introduced pests (b) Slow-breeding (c) Both above (d) Not known

613. Name the largest eagle of Europe which has become locally extinct owing to poisoning and egg collection:

(a) Bald Eagle (*Haliaeetus leucocephalus*) (b) Sea Eagle (*Haliaeetus albicilla*) (c) Wandering Albatross (*Diomedia exulans*) (d) Tawny Eagle (*Aquila rapax vindhiana*)

614. How many species of the albatross are to be found in the world?

(a) 2 (b) 4 (c) 10 (d) 14

615. To which country is the bee hummingbird (*Mellisuga helenae*) endemic?

(a) India (b) Canada (c) Brazil (d) Cuba

616. What is the estimated beat of the hummingbird's wings per second?

(a) 50 (b) 60 (c) 70 (d) 80

617. What is the main reason of the colony-wise nesting among birds, termed as *colonial nesting* in ornithology.

(a) Shortage of suitable nest sites (b) Safety of parents, eggs and chicks in colonies (c) Both above (d) Not known

618. Who said '... the spectrum of India's birdlife is truly fabulous. It seems almost unbelievable that one can identify over a hundred species of birds within an hour in almost any garden, forest, bushland or patch of open savanna anywhere in India'?

(a) Dr. Salim Ali (b) S. Dillon Ripley (c) Kailash Sankhala (d) David Attenborough

619. What is the state bird of Hawaii?

(a) Quetzal (*Pharomachrus mocino*) (b) Scarlet Ibis (*Eudocimus ruber*) (c) Nene Goose (*Branta sandvicensis*) (d) Redvented Rulbul (*Pycnonotus cafer*)

620. Which bird is the national symbol of Trinidad and Tobago?

(a) Quetzal (*Pharomachrus mocino*) (b) Scarlet Ibis (*Eudocimus ruber*) (c) Nene Goose (*Branta sandvicensis*) (d) Redvented Rulbul (*Pycnonotus cafer*)

8
THE REPTILES

621. What is a reptile?

(a) Creeping animal (b) Arboreal animal (c) Omnivorus animal (d) Large animal

622. How many species of reptiles are to be found in the world?

(a) 500 (b) 6,000 (c) 10,000 (d) 12,000

623. Name the snake which provides a traditional delicacy at wedding feasts in Papua New Guinea:

(a) Paradise Flying Snake (*Chrysopelea pelias*)
(b) Green Python (*Chondropython viridis*)
(c) Gold's Cobra (*Pseudonaje goldii*)
(d) Boomslang (*Dispholidus typus*)

624. What is the preferred habitat of the green python (*Chondrophython viridis*)

(a) Deserts (b) Rain forests (c) Ocean (d) Caves

625. What is the distribution of the green python (*Chondropython viridis*)?

(a) New Guinea, Solomons and Aru Islands and Australia (b) India, Nepal and Bhutan (c) North America (d) South America

626. Which snake is also known as the Hamadryad?

(a) Reticulated Python (*Python reticulatus*) (b) King Cobra (*Ophiophagus hannah*) (c) Indian Python (*Python molurus*) (d) Black Mamba (*Dendroapsis polylepis*)

627. What is the method of the pythons to obtain food?

(a) Coiling around the victim to crush it and obstruct breathing (b) Swallow the killed animal (c) Bite and inject venom (d) Both (a) and (b)

628. How many species of pythons are to be found in the world?

(a) 10 (b) 16 (c) 21 (d) 25

629. What is the aerial movement of a flying snake called?

(a) Flight (b) Gliding (c) Crawling (d) Running

630. Generally, snakes do not have limbs and legs, but some species still retain internal relics of their hip bones and have spurs on either side of the vent. Name it:

(a) Cobras (b) Pythons and Boas (c) Vipers (d) Rattlesnakes

631. Where is the paradise flying snake (*Chrysopelea pelias*) to be found?

(a) Borneo (b) Galapagos (c) Sri Lanka (d) Canada

632. What is the preferred habitat of the paradise flying snake (*Chrysopelea pelias*)?

(a) Forests (b) Sand dunes (c) Rivers (d) Caves

633. Which of the following snakes are capable of gliding through the air?

(a) Golden Tree Snake (*Chrysopelea ornata*)
(b) Paradise Flying Snake (*Chrysopelea pelias*)
(c) Andaman Flying Snake (*Chrysopelea paradisi*) (d) All the above

634. What is the food of a paradise flying snake (*Chrysopelea pelias*)?

(a) Lizards and tree skins (b) Fruits (c) Eggs (d) Seeds

635. Which non-venomous harmless snake in India is mistaken for the venomous cobra (*Naja naja*)?

(a) Common Green Mamba (*Dendroapsis anguisticeps*) (b) Common Wolf Snake (*Lycodon aulicus*) (c) Common Kukri Snake (*Oligodon arnensis*) (d) Rat Snake (*Elaphe obsoleta*)

636. What is the method of self-defence used by the grass snake (*Natrix natrix*)?

(a) Release of bad-smelling chemicals of stink glands (b) In extreme cases shams dead (c) Fast crawling (d) Both (a) and (b)

637. What is the preferred habitat of the snake sidewinder (*Crotalus cerastes*)?

(a) Rain forests (b) Oceans (c) Sandy deserts (d) Wetlands

638. Where is the sidewinder (*Crotalus cerastes*) found?

(a) Western North America (b) Thar Desert (c) Sahara Desert (d) Kenya

639. How does the sidewinder (*Crotalus cerastes*) move?

(a) Sidewinding (Sideways movement) (b) Crawling (c) Both above (d) Not defined

640. Is the sidewinder (*Crotalus cerastes*) a venomous snake?

(a) Yes (b) No

641. Does the sidewinder (*Crotalus cerastes*) give birth directly to young ones and not by the usual egg-laying of snakes?

(a) Yes (b) No

642. Is the horned viper (*Cerastes cerastes*) a poisonous snake?

(a) Yes (b) No

643. What is the locational distribution of the horned viper (*Cerastes cerastes*)?

(a) Western U.S.A. (b) South America (c) North Africa and Arabia (d) Asia

101

644. A group of islands in Indian Ocean, off the coast of East Africa, are famous for some 150,000 giant tortoises. Name it:

(a) Aleutian Islands (b) Aldabra Islands (c) Andaman Islands (d) Nicobar Islands

645. What are the adaptations of the horned viper (*Cerastes cerastes*) to desert life?

(a) Rough scaling for hold on sand (b) Thick skin to reduce moisture loss (c) Both above (d) No adaptations

646. Which of the following snakes are to be found in deserts?

(a) Sidewinder (*Crotalus cerastes*) (b) Saw-scaled Viper (*Echis carinatus*) (c) Horned Viper (*Cerastes cerastes*) (d) All the above

647. What is the common name for the adder (*Vipera berus*)?

(a) Common Viper (b) Cobra (c) Anaconda (d) Krait

648. How does the adder (*Vipera berus*) obtain its food?

(a) Strike prey from cover when it is passing by and inject the venom Neurotoxin (b) Follow the stricken animal until its death (c) Swallowing the killed animal (d) All above

649. What is the food of the adder (*Vipera berus*)?

(a) Lizards and small mammals (b) Insects (c) Fruits (d) All the above

650. What is the usage of the 'pit' in the pit viper?

(a) Heat-sensor (b) It helps in locating warm blooded prey (c) Both above (d) Not known

651. How many species of rattlesnakes are to be found in the world?

(a) 10 (b) 20 (c) 30 (d) 40

652. Which part of the body is used to produce the rattlesnake's rattling?

(a) Tail (b) Mouth (c) Tail and Mouth (d) Ribs

653. What is the food of the rattlesnake?

(a) Grass-roots (b) Rodents, small mammals (c) Fruits (d) Ants

654. (a) Is it true that rattlesnakes do not lay eggs but give birth to fully developed young?

(a) Yes (b) No

655. What is the common name of the common African tree snake (*Dispholidus typus*)?

(a) Boomslang (b) Adder (c) Hamadryad (d) Mamba

656. Which is the largest snake?

(a) Anaconda (b) Reticulated Python (c) King Cobra (d) Viper

657. What is the preferred habitat of the South African snake anaconda (*Eunectes murinus*)?

(a) Swamps and river (b) Forests (c) Deserts (d) Caves

658. What is the body size of the anaconda (*Eunectes murinus*)?

(a) 60 cm length, 10 cm girth (b) 2 m length, 25 cm girth (c) 9 m length, 1 m girth (d) 10 m length, 1 m girth

659. What is the food of the adult anaconda (*Eunectes murinus*)?

(a) Small deer, monkeys, goats and wild boar (b) Rodents and water birds (c) Both above (d) Not known

660. Which is the largest (not the longest) reptile in the world?

(a) Anaconda (*Eunectes murinus*) (b) Reticulated Python (*Python reticulatus*) (c) King Cobra (*Ophiophagus hannah*) (d) Hind Viper (*Vipera hindi*)

661. Which is the longest reptile in the world?

(a) Anaconda (*Eunectes murinus*) (b) Reticulated Python (*Python reticulatus*) (c) King Cobra (*Ophiophagus hannah*) (d) Hind Viper (*Vipera hindi*)

662. Is the anaconda (*Eunectes murinus*) a venomous snake?

(a) Yes (b) No

663. How does the anaconda (*Eunectes murinus*) kill its prey?

(a) Killing by coiling and crushing to suffocate the prey and swallowing whole body (b) Killing by venomous bite (c) Both above (d) Not recorded

664. Where is the anaconda (*Eunectes murinus*) found?

(a) Northern South America, mostly Amazon (b) India (c) Africa (d) Europe

665. How does the boa constrictor (*Boa constrictor*) kill its prey?

(a) Coiling around the prey, constriction, suffocation and swallowing whole (b) Venomous bite (c) Both above (d) Not known

666. What is the range of distribution of the Jamaica boa (*Epicrates subflavus*)?

(a) Asia (b) Africa (c) Australia (d) Jamaica and Goat Islands in Caribbean

667. What is the preferred habitat of the Jamaica boa (*Epicrates subflavus*)?

(a) Rain forests (b) Swamps (c) Caves (d) Rockey areas and scrubland

668. What is the reason for the threat to the Jamaica boa (*Epicrates subflavus*)?

(a) Predation by introduced mongooses (b) Predation by feral cats (c) Killing for skin (d) Only (a) and (b)

669. (a) Most of the boas are becoming endangered. What is the reason?

(a) Predation by introduced mongooses and feral cats on islands (b) Collection for pet-trade and oil (c) Habitat destruction (d) All the above

670. Which of the following species of the boa is threatened with extinction?

(a) Jamaica Boa (b) Puerto Rican Boa (c) Cuban Boa (d) Round Island Boa (e) All the above

671. What is the length of the Jamaica boa (*Epicrates subflavus*)?

(a) 60 cm (b) 1 m (c) 1.5 m (d) 2 m

672. How many species of sea-snakes are to be found in the world?

(a) 10 (b) 50 (c) 100 (d) 200

673. Is it true that most of the sea-snakes are highly poisonous?

(a) Yes (b) No

674. How do sea-snakes obtain food?

(a) Coiling, constriction and suffocation (b) Striking, biting, venom injection (c) Both above (d) Not known

675. What is the main chemical constituent of the snake venom?

(a) Carbohydrate (b) Protein (c) Vitamins (d) Minerals

676. What are the local symptoms of a bite by a venomous snake?

(a) Pain (b) Immediate swelling (c) Blisters and necrosis (d) All the above

677. Is it true that discoloration of the skin around the bite occurs in the case of a cobra (*Naja naja*), King Cobra (*Ophiophagus hannah*) and a viper (*Vipera* sp.) bite?

(a) Yes (b) No

678. If severe abdominal pain is noticed in the victim of a snake-bite, which is the snake most likely associated with the bite?

(a) Krait (b) King Cobra (c) Cobra (d) Mamba

679. What is the most important symptom of the viper bite in the human being?

(a) Burning and stinging pain at the bite point (b) Constant bleeding from bite point (c) Local swelling (d) All the above

680. What first aid should be given to a victim of a snake-bite?

(a) Wipe the bite point with clean water and cover it with a clean bandage (b) Application of firm ligature with a cloth or bandage above the bite point (c) Shift the casualty to the nearest hospital (d) All the above

681. How many species of lizards are to be found in the world?

(a) 1,000 (b) 2,000 (c) 3,000 (d) 4,000

682. How do lizards avoid being overheated in the deserts?

(a) Shelter in shade (b) Raise the belly off the ground (c) Ability to survive with higher body temperature (d) All the above

683. Which is the largest lizard in the world?

(a) Komodo Dragon (*Varanus komodensis*), Indonesia (b) Perentie (*Varanus giganteus*), Australia (c) Water Monitor *(Varanus salvator)*, India (d) Giant Plated Lizard (*Gerrhosaurus major*) Brazil

684. Which is the second largest lizard in the world?

(a) Perentie *(Varanus giganteus)* (b) Water Monitor *(Varanus salvator)* (c) Both above are contenders for the title (d) Not known

685. What is the length of the komodo dragon *(Varanus komodensis)*?

(a) 1 m (b) 2 m (c) 3 m (d) 4 m

686. What is the weight of the adult komodo dragon?

(a) 50 Kg (b) 75 Kg (c) 135 Kg (d) 200 Kg

687. What is the preferred habitat of the komodo dragon *(Varanus komodensis)*?

(a) Rain forests (b) Deserts (c) Island savannah (d) Caves

688. What is the adaptation required of a monitor lizard, dragon and snake for swallowing its prey whole?

(a) They can increase the size of the mouth by dislocating the lower jaw (b) By inflating body (c) Both above (d) No adaptation

689. What constitutes the prey of the komodo dragon (*Varanus komodensis*)?

(a) Adults prey on wild pigs, deer and domesticated goats (b) Young feed on insects and smaller mammals (c) Carrion (d) All the above

690. What is the reason for the threat to the komodo dragon (*Varanus komodensis*)?

(a) Commercial exploitation for skin (b) Direct killing by people as it preys on domesticated pigs and goats (c) Hunting of its prey animals by men and habitat destruction (d) All the above

691. What physical adaptation does the thorny devil (*Moloch horridus*) possess for its self-protection?

(a) Body covered with spikes (b) Stink glands (c) Poison (d) All the above

692. What is the food of the desert-dwelling lizard thorny devil (*Moloch horridus*)?

(a) Ants (b) Rats (c) Deer (d) Fruits

693. Which lizard in India is threatened with extinction due to over-exploitation for its fat, allegedly thought to be an aphrodisiac, and its tail for food?

(a) Coast Horned Lizard (*Phrynosoma coronatum*) (b) Spiny-tailed Lizard (*Uromastyx hardwickii*) (c) Flying Lizard (*Draco dussumieri*) (d) All the above

694. Where is the marine iguana (*Amblyrhynchus cristatus*) found?

(a) Australia (b) Galapagos Islands (c) Africa (d) India

695. What is the preferred habitat of the marine iguana (*Amblyrhynchus cristatus*)?

(a) Marine rocky coasts (b) Deserts (c) Alpine scrub (d) Rain forests

696. What constitute the food of marine iguana (*Amblyrhynchus cristatus*)?

(a) Small mammals (b) Marine fish (c) Algae and seaweeds (d) All the above

697. What is the principal cause for threat to the marine iguana (*Amblyrhynchus cristatus*)?

(a) Direct persecution (b) Habitat destruction (c) Introduced feral dogs and cats on islands (d) All the above

698. What is the main difference between alligators and crocodiles?

(a) The alligator has 17 to 22 teeth on each side of its jaw but the crocodile has only 14 to 15 (b) In the alligator the fourth tooth on each side of the lower jaw fits into a corresponding pit in the upper jaw; it is not so in the case of a crocodile, hence its teeth are always visible (c) Both the above

699. What are the threats to the survival of the American alligator (*Alligator mississippiensis*)?

(a) Destruction of marshy lakes (b) Hunting for skin (c) Egg collection (d) Only (a) and (b)

700. The total population of the American alligator (*Alligator mississippiensis*) in the world is estimated to be about 800,000 after proper management and conservation. What is the management strategy followed?

(a) Habitat protection (b) Ban on harvesting
(c) Both the above (d) None of the above

701. What is the colour of the eggs of crocodiles and alligators?

(a) White (b) Blue (c) Brown (d) Green

702. Which is the largest crocodile in the world?

(a) Marsh Crocodile (*Crocodylus palustris*) (b) Gharial (*Gavialis gangeticus*) (c) Estuarine Crocodile (*Crocodylus porosus*) (d) Nile Crocodile (*Crocodylus niloticus*)

703. What is the food habit of crocodiles and alligators?

(a) Herbivorous (b) Carnivorous (c) Omnivorous (d) Frugivorous

704. What is the cause for the depletion and threat to the mugger (*Crocodylus palustris*) in India?

(a) Commercial hunting for skin (b) Habitat loss (c) Egg collection (d) All the above

705. What is the cause for extinction of the salt-water crocodile (*Crocodylus porosus*) over a large range of its former locations?

(a) Hunting for skin (b) Loss of breeding habitat (c) Both the above (d) None of the above

706. How is the gharial or long-snouted crocodile (*Gavialis gangeticus*) distinguished from the marsh and estuarine crocodiles?

(a) Gharial has a long snout (b) Gharial is a fish-eater (c) Both the above (d) No difference

707. In India, hunting for its skin and loss of habitat due to damming of rivers have adversely affected the population of the

gharial (*Gavialis gangeticus*). What was the management strategy followed to help conserve this species?

(a) Egg collection from wild, captive rearing and release into the wild (b) Ban on hunting (c) Habitat conservation (d) All the above

708. How many species of crocodile are found in Africa?

(a) 2 (b) 3 (c) 4 (d) 6

709. Name the largest African crocodile:

(a) Nile Crocodile (*Crocodylus niloticus*) (b) Long-snouted Crocodile (*C. cataphractus*) (c) Broad-fronted or Dwarf Crocodile (*Osteolaemous tetraspis*) (d) Both (a) and (b) have the same length

710. What is the cause for depletion and threat to the crocodiles in Africa?

(a) Habitat destruction (b) Over-exploitation (c) Both (a) and (b) (d) Not known

711. What is the nest-site selected by the Nile crocodile (*Crocodylus niloticus*)?

(a) Riverside flats, low-lying islets (b) Sandy lake-side beaches and bed of the dried watercourse (c) Both the above

712. Name the predator that destroys the eggs of the Nile crocodile (*Crocodylus niloticus*)?

(a) Nile Monitor (b) Olive Baboon (c) Spotted Hyaena, Ratel and White-tailed Mongoose and some birds (d) All the above

713. Which is the smallest marine turtle?

(a) Loggerhead (*Caretta caretta*) (b) Green Turtle (*Chelonia mydas*) (c) Olive Ridley Turtle

(*Lepidochelys olivacea*) (d) Hawksbill Turtle (*Eretmochelys imbricata*)

714. What is the nest-site of the sea turtles?

(a) Beaches with light sand (b) Island forests (c) Deep sea (d) All the above

715. What kind of nest is prepared by the green turtle (*Chelonia mydas*)?

(a) Vegetation mound (b) Sand pit (c) Pebble mound (d) Flat platform

716. What is the curious nesting behaviour of the Olive Ridley turtle (*Lepidochelys olivacea*)?

(a) Nest covering with vegetation (b) Open nests (c) Both the above (d) Under water nesting

717. Name the most valuable of all living reptiles exploited for its meat, soup, eggs and oil:

(a) Hawksbill Turtle (*Eretmochelys imbricata*) (b) Green Turtle (*Chelonia mydas*) (c) Loggerhead Turtle (*Caretta caretta*) (d) All sea turtles

718. What is the difference between land tortoises and terrapins?

(a) Terrapins have flattened limbs and webbed digits (b) Terrapins are aquatic (c) Both the above (d) Terrapins have outer shell

719. What is the cause for the threat to the giant tortoise (*Geochelone elephantopus*) in the Galapagos Islands?

(a) Exploitation for meat (b) Competition for food with domestic cattles, donkeys and goats of settlers (c) Both the above (d) Climatic change

720. What is the nest-site selected by the giant tortoise (*Geochelone elephantopus*)?

(a) Bare patch on the ground (b) Pit nest (c) Twig nest (d) Cavity nest

721. What is the food of the giant tortoise (*Geochelone elephantopus*)?

(a) Vegetation (b) Fish (c) Insects (d) Snakes

722. What threats are destroying the nesting habitat of the loggerhead turtle (*Caretta caretta*)?

(a) Beach tourism (b) Beach construction (hotels, etc.) (c) Both the above (d) Tides

723. How many species of sea turtles are to be found in the world?

(a) 5 (b) 6 (c) 7 (d) 8

724. Of seven species of sea turtles in the world, how many are endangered?

(a) 5 (b) 6 (c) 7 (d) 4

725. What strategy is followed for the conservation of sea turtles in India?

(a) Controlling exploitation (b) Habitat and nest-site protection (c) Egg collection from the wild, incubation and hatching and return to the wild (d) All the above

726. Name the largest turtle in the world:

(a) Green Turtle (*Chelonia mydas*) (b) Pacific Ridley Turtle (*Lepidochelys olivacea*) (c) Leatherback Turtle (*Dermochelys coriacea*) (d) Nile Soft-shelled

727. Name the smallest sea turtle in the world:

(a) Green Turtle (*Chelonia mydas*) (b) Pacific Ridley Turtle (*Lepidochelys olivacea*)

(c) Leather-back Turtle (*Dermochelys coriacea*)
(d) Nile Soft-shelled

728. Which is the most endangered lizard in the world?

(a) **Black Legless Lizard** (*Anniella pulchra nigra*), **California** (b) Reticulate Gila Monster (*Heloderma suspectum*) (c) Blunt-nosed Leopard Lizard or San Joaquin Leopard Lizard (*Grotaphytus wislizenii*) (d) Giant Plated Lizard (*Gerrhosaurus major*)

729. What is the cause for the threat of extinction to the leopard lizard (*Grotaphytus wislizenii*) of California?

(a) Killing (b) Predation (c) **Conversion of arid San Joaquin Valley into farmlands** (d) Predation and killing

730. Why is the rhinoceros iguana (*Cyclura cornuta cornuta*) so named?

(a) Big body size (b) **Presence of hornlike spurs above the nostrils** (c) Thick skin (d) All the above

731. Which of the following snakes are threatened with extinction?

(a) Madagascar Boa (*Acrantophis dumerili*) (b) San Francisco Garter Snake (*Thamnophis sirtalis*) (c) **Both the above** (d) Cobra (*Naja naja*)

732. How many species of turtles are to be found in the world?

(a) 5 (b) 6 (c) 7 (d) 9

733. What is the state reptile of California?

(a) Green Turtle (*Chelonia mydas*) (b) **Desert Tortoise** (*Gopherus agassizi*) (c) Giant Tortoise

(Geochelone elephantopus) (d) Pancake Tortoise
(Malachochersus torneiri)

9
THE AMPHIBIANS

734. What is understood by 'amphibia'?

(a) Animals that can survive both on land and water (b) Animals with long tail (c) Animals with short nose (d) All the above

735. To which broad group do frogs belong?

(a) Fish (b) Reptilia (c) Mammalia (d) Amphibia

736. To which group do toads belong?

(a) Fish (b) Amphibia (c) Reptilia (d) Mammalia

737. To which group do salamanders belong?

(a) Fish (b) Amphibia (c) Reptilia (d) Mammalia

738. What is the distribution of arrow poison frogs?

(a) Africa (b) Central and South America (c) Asia (d) Australia

739. How is the poison from the body of the arrow poison frogs obtained by native South Americans?

(a) Frogs are held over a flame and the poison that oozes out collected (b) Frogs are dissected to collect poison (c) Poison is collected from the skin (d) Poison is collected from eyes

740. What is the egg-laying site selected by frogs?
(a) Fresh water (b) Marine water (c) Ground
(d) Tree leaves

741. How many species of frogs and toads are to
be found in the world?
(a) 1,200 (b) 2,600 (c) 4,000 (d) 5,000

742. How do frogs breathe?
(a) Through gills in tadpole stage
(b) Through lungs and skin in adult stage
(c) Both the above (d) Not known

743. What is the difference in the movement of
frogs and toads?
(a) Frogs move by jumping (b) Toads normally move by crawling (c) Both the above
(d) Frogs move by running

744. What is the difference in the skin of frogs
and toads?
(a) Frogs have moist and slippery skin
(b) Toads have dry and warty skin (c) Both
the above (d) No difference

745. How many species of frogs are found in
Madagascar?
(a) 40 (b) 50 (c) 100 (d) 150

746. Name the only representative of tailed
amphibia in India:
(a) Ceylon Bull Frog (*Kaloula pulchra*) (b) Indian Bull Frog (*Rana tigrina*) (c) Indian Newt
(*Tylototriton verrucosus*) (d) Alpine Salamander
(*Salamandra atra*)

747. What is the way in which the tree frogs move?
(a) Running (b) Jumping (c) Crawling
(d) Gliding

748. Normally frogs and salamanders depend on water but some amphibians found in very high altitudes do not need water and are completely terrestrial. Name one such species:

(a) Alpine Salamander (*Salamandra altra*)
(b) Tree Frog (*Raccophorus reinwardtii*)
(c) Green Frog (*Rana clamitans*) (d) Ceylon Bull Frog (*Kaloula pulchra*)

749. What is the effect of wetland drainage and pollution of fresh water lakes on the amphibians?

(a) Death (b) Non-availability of breeding site
(c) Both the above (d) Migration

750. Name the frog found only in a three square mile of protected area — El Valie de Anton:

(a) Panamanian Golden Frog (*Atelopus varius zeteki*) (b) Pine Barrens tree frog (*Hyla andersoni*) (c) Seychelle Island frog (*Nesomantis thomasseti*) (d) Tree Frog (*Raccophorus reinwardtii*)

751. Name the toad found only in 5 hectares of land near Death Valley in California:

(a) Black Toad (*Bufo boreas exsul*) (b) Sonoran Green Toad (*Bufo retiformis*) (c) Mount Nimba Viviparous Toad (*Nectophrynoides occidentalis*) (d) Firebellied Toad (*Bombina orientalis*)

752. What is the cause for the depletion and threat to the Black Toad (*Bufo boreas exsul*) found near Death Valley in California?

(a) Drainage and canalization of breeding streams (b) Collection (c) Predation (d) All the above

753. Name the American salamander found only in Ezell's Cave near San Marcos in Texas

that, unlike other members of the group, retains gills throughout its life for breathing: (a) Chinese Giant Salamander (*Andrias davidianus*) (b) Texas Blind Salamander (*Typhlomolge rathbuni*) (c) Goldstriped Salamander (*Chioglossa lusitanica*) (d) Alpine Salamander (*Salamandra atra*)

754. Which is the largest amphibian in the world? (a) Chinese Giant Salamander (*Andrias davidianus*) (b) Texas Blind Salamander (*Typhlomolge rathbuni*) (c) Goldstriped Salamander (*Chioglossa lusitanica*) (d) Alpine Salamander (*Salamandra atra*)

755. What is the cause for the depletion and threat to the Chinese giant salamander (*Andrias davidianus*)?
(a) Collection as pets (b) Harvest for food (c) Habitat loss (d) All the above

756. Which is the most venomous amphibian in the world?
(a) Arrow-poison Frog (*Dendrobates* spp.), South America (b) Mud-puddle Frog (*Physalaemus pustulosus*), Panama (c) Fire-bellied Toad (*Bombina orientalis*), East Asia (d) Chinese Giant Salamander (*Andrias davidianus*)

757. What is the lethal dose of poison for man, obtained from the Arrow-poison Frog (*Dendrobates* spp.)?
(a) $\frac{1}{10,000}$ gram (b) $\frac{1}{100}$ gram (c) 1 gram (d) 2 grams

10
THE FISHES

758. Name the most venomous fish in the world:
(a) Stone Fish (*Synanceia horrida*) (b) Whale Shark (*Rhincodon typus*) (c) Bombay Duck (*Harpodon nehereus*) (d) Hilsa (*Hilsa hilsa*)

759. Which fish is used as a decoy to trap dolphins?
(a) Hilsa (*Hilsa hilsa*) (b) Climbing Perch (*Anabas testudineus*) (c) Striped Marlin (*Tetrappturus brevirostris*) (d) Stone Fish (*Synanceia horrida*)

760. Which is the most restricted fish in the world, found only in a pool in Navada in western U.S.A.?
(a) Devil's hole Pupfish (*Cyprinodon diabolis*) (b) Desert Pupfish (*C. macularius*) (c) Hilsa (*Hilsa hilsa*) (d) Climbing Perch (*Anabas testudineus*)

761. To which group of animals do sharks belong?
(a) Reptiles (b) Fish (c) Mammals (d) Amphibians

762. All the species of fish have a unique water pressure detecting system. What is it called?
(a) Lateral line system (b) Ventral line system (c) Darsal line system (d) Inner line system

763. What is the food of a scorpionfish (*Pterois* sp.)?
(a) Crabs and shrimps (b) Grass (c) Sea-weed (d) All the above

764. How many species of parrotfish (*Scaridae*) are to be found in the world?
(a) 10 (b) 30 (c) 50 (d) 80

765. Why is the parrotfish so named?

(a) Presence of 'beaks' formed by teeth (b) It has a bill (c) It has two bills

766. For what purpose is the 'beak' of a parrotfish used?

(a) Killing the enemy (b) Scraping corals (c) Chewing (d) All the above

767. Which fish causes enormous damage to the coral reef during its feeding?

(a) Parrotfish (b) Shark (c) Marlin (d) Scorpionfish

768. What is a popular name of the scorpionfish?

(a) Zebrafish (b) Dragonfish (c) Devilfish (d) All the above

769. What is the habitat of the striped marlin (*Terapturus audax*)?

(a) Freshwater rivers (b) Deep sea (c) Both the above (d) Estuaries

770. Sharks and rays cannot perceive colour. Why?

(a) Lack of cone cells in the eyes (b) Lack of rods in the eyes (c) Lack of rods and cones in the eyes (d) Presence of cones and rods in the eyes

771. Why is the butterfly fish (*Chaetodon*) so named?

(a) It looks like a butterfly (b) It has varied colours (c) It can fly (d) It has wings

772. A fish was thought to be extinct 70 million years ago; it was rediscovered in the year 1938 off the mouth of the Chalumna river. Name it:

(a) Pla Buk (*Pangasianodon gigas*)
(b) Coelacanth (*Latimeria chalumnae*) (c) Dwarf
Gobi (*Trimmaton nanus*) (d) Hilsa (*Hilsa hilsa*)

773. Identify the sea animal which does not swim
with its body held horizontally, instead it
keeps itself vertical under water:
(a) Amazon Knife fish (*Stonarchus albifrons*)
(b) Guppy (*Poecilia reticulata*) (c) Sea-horses
(*Hipocampus*) (d) Sardine (*Sardinops caeruleus*)

774. In which species of animals does the male,
after copulation, induce the female to deposit
her eggs into the pouch in the male body,
and finally gives birth to the young ones after
about two weeks time?
(a) Amazon Knife fish (*Stonarchus albifrons*)
(b) Guppy (*Poecilia reticulata*) (c) Sea-horses
(*Hipocampus*) (d) Sardine (*Sardinops caeruleus*)

775. The easiest way to save an over-exploited
species from extinction is to stop commercial
harvest. However, a fish population in
California has failed to recover even after
the protection over five decades. Name the
species:
(a) Sardine (*Sardinops caeruleus*) (b) Goldfish
(*Carassius auratus*) (c) Roach (*Rutilus rutilus*)
(d) Guppy (*Poecilia reticulata*)

776. Name the exotic fish that poses a danger to
the survival of the viviparous fish (*Gambusia
gaigei*) found in the Big Bend National Park
of Texas:
(a) Maluti (*Oreodaimon quathlambae*) (b) Goldfish (*Carassius auratus*) (c) Mosquito Fish
(*Gambusia affinis*) (d) Emperor Fish
(*Scleropagas formosus*)

11

INSECTS AND OTHER
INVERTEBRATES

777. The bush cricket normally produces sound by rubbing its wings together. Name the cricket that makes a sound by beating the ground with one hind leg:
    (a) Swallowtail Butterfly (*Papilio machaon*)
    (b) Oak Bush Cricket (*Meconema thalassinum*)
    (c) Silk Moth (*Bombyx mori*) (d) Dung Beetle (*Scarabaeus sacer*)

778. Name the largest butterfly in Great Britain:
    (a) Swallowtail Butterfly (*Papilio machaon*)
    (b) Birdwint Butterfly (*Ornithopteria allottei*)
    (c) Alexandra Birdwing Butterfly (*O alexandrae*) (d) Large Blue Butterfly (*Maculinea arion*)

779. What is the cause for the disappearance of the swallowtail butterfly from its former range of occurrence?
    (a) Trapping (b) Wetland drainage (c) Predation (d) All the above

780. Which one of the following insects is not found in the wild?
    (a) Swallowtail Butterfly (*Papilio machaon*)
    (b) Oak Bush Cricket (*Meconema thalassinum*)
    (c) Silk Moth (*Bombyx mori*) (d) All the above

781. What is a katydid?
    (a) Insect (b) Frog (c) Fish (d) Snake

782. How many species of the birdwing butterfly are to be found in the world?
    (a) 4 (b) 8 (c) 10 (d) 12

783. Name the largest butterfly in the world:

(a) Birdwing Butterfly (*Ornithopteria allottei*)
(b) Alexandra Birdwing Butterfly (*Ornithopteria alexandrae*) (c) Swallowtail Butterfly (*Papilio machaon*) (d) Mycalesia (*Mycalesia rama*)

784. What is the wing span of the Alexandra birdwing butterfly (*Ornithopteria alexandrae*) found in New Guinea?

(a) 25 cm (b) 26 cm (c) 27 cm (d) 28 cm

785. What is the range of distribution of birdwing butterflies in the world?

(a) Australia (b) South America (c) Africa (d) South-east Asia

786. Which is the rarest butterfly in the world?

(a) Birdwing Butterfly (*Ornithopteria allottei*)
(b) Purple Emperor (*Apatura iris*) (c) Monarch Butterfly (*Danaus plexippus*) (d) Mycalesia (*Mycalesia rama*)

787. An insect performs migrations twice every year. It overwinters in California and Mexico but breeds about 3000 kilometres north of its wintering grounds. Name it:

(a) Birdwing Butterfly (*Ornithopleria allottei*)
(b) Purple Emperor (*Apatura iris*) (c) Monarch Butterfly (*Danaus plexippus*) (d) Mycalesia (*Mycalesia rama*)

788. Though monarch butterfly (*Danaus plexippus*) are found in the millions, yet it is endangered. For what reasons?

(a) Known roosts in North America face threat from logging, tourism and grazing (b) Tourism induced forest fires (c) Both the above (d) Not known

789. Name the butterfly that inhabits the northernmost latitude:

(a) Arctic Fritillary Butterfly (*Clossiana chariclea*) (b) Mycalesia Butterfly (*Mycalesia rama*) (c) Large Blue Butterfly (*Maculinea arion*) (d) Purple Emperor (*Apatura iris*)

790. Name the largest moth in existence found in south-east Asia:

(a) Atlas Moth (*Attacus atlas*) (b) Pine Hawk Moth (*Hyloicus pinastri*) (c) Elephant Hawk Moth (*Deilephila elpenor*) (d) Silk Moth (*Bombyx mori*)

791. Which chemical is emitted by the female moth to attract the male moths during the mating season?

(a) Melanin (b) Sugar (c) Pheromon (d) Adrenalin

792. How many species of spiders are to be found in the world?

(a) 10,000 (b) 20,000 (c) 30,000 (d) 40,000

793. How many species of bird-eating spiders are to be found in the world?

(a) 300 (b) 400 (c) 500 (d) 600

794. How many species of beetles are there in the world?

(a) 1,300 (b) 3,000 (c) 30,000 (d) 300,000

795. Which is the largest beetle in the world?

(a) Goliath Beetle (*Goliathus gigantus*) (b) Dung Beetle (*Scarabaeus sacer*) (c) Stag Beetle (*Lucanus cervus*) (d) Dak Bush Cricket (*Meconema thalassinum*)

796. How many species of scorpions are to be found in the world?

(a) 200 (b) 300 (c) 400 (d) 600

797. What is the food of the scorpions?
(a) Leaves and grass (b) Beetles and cock-roaches (c) Seeds (d) Flower petals

798. Name the scorpion found in the Sahara Desert that can kill medium-sized mammals:
(a) *Androctonus australis* (b) *Heterometrus swammerdami* (c) *Microbothus pusillus*

799. Which is the largest crab in the world?
(a) Robbe Crab (*Birgus latro*) (b) Coconut crab (c) (a) and (b) are synonyms

800. What is unique about the Californian petroleum fly (*Psilopa petrolei*)?
(a) It yields petroleum (b) It is a fossil (c) Its larvae live in pools of crude oil (d) It eats petroleum

801. Which beetle instinctively rolls balls of dung to use these either for food or for laying eggs?
(a) Seven-spot Ladybird (*Coccinella septempunctata*) (b) Goliath Beetle (*Goliathus giganteus*) (c) Tumblebug (*Scarabaeus sacer*) (d) Stag Beetle (*Lucanus cervus*)

802. If you want to attract butterflies in your garden, which special technique would you follow?
(a) Chrysalids obtained from a butterfly-farm are put in the garden to hatch (b) Grow nectar and fragrance bearing flowering plants (c) Both the above (d) No technique

803. Which animal produces the largest number of eggs — one thousand million — at a time?

(a) Giant Damsefly (*Megaloprepus coerulatus*)
(b) Land Crab (*Gecarcoidea natalus*)
(c) Tumblebug (*Scarabaeus sacer*) (d) Giant Clam (*Tridacna*)

804. Various breeding strategies have evolved among the animals like corals, seaurchins and jellyfish to carry on their species. Some produce eggs numbering millions and leave them to struggle and survive on their own; some, like the birds and reptiles, provide rich yolk for the initial development of the hatching and look after their young ones. What strategy is adopted by insects for survival of young ones?

(a) Egg laying near the rich source of natural food (b) Parental care (c) Eggs with rich yolk (d) All the above

805. Insects normally lay eggs but there are exceptions where they give birth to young ones? Name these exceptions:

(a) Bot fly (*Oestridae* and *Gasterophilidae*)
(b) Tsetse Fly (*Glossina* sp.) (c) Both the above
(d) No exception

806. Owing to the drainage of fens and over-collecting, a butterfly became extinct in England in 1848. However, a newly discovered subspecies from the Netherlands was successfully reintroduced in 1927 at Woodwalton fen. Name this butterfly:

(a) Large Copper Butterfly (*Lycaena dispar*)
(b) Monarch Butterfly (*Danaus plexippus*)
(c) Large Blue Butterfly (*Maculinea arion*)
(d) Arctic Firitillary (*Clossiana chariclea*)

807. What is the most preferred food, a very poisonous plant, of the Monarch Butterfly (*Danaus plexippus*)?

(a) Deadly Nightshade (*Atropa belladonna*) (b) Milkweed (*Asclepias*) (c) Poison Ivy (*Rhus toxicodendron*) (d) Neem (*Azadirachta indica*)

808. What is the chemical nature of the spider web?

(a) Sugar (b) Vitamin (c) Fat (d) Protein

809. The world's largest terrestrial snail is over 15 cm in length. Name it:

(a) Giant African Snail (*Achatina fulica*) (b) Cannibal Snail (*Euglandina rosea*) (c) Roman Snail (*Helix pomatia*) (d) Hylothid

810. Sometimes ecological studies and experiments bring unknown disaster to wild animals. A species of moth has the unique distinction of being the first animal known to have become extinct in the course of a field study, in 1980. Name this moth:

(a) Scarlet Tiger Moth (*Panaxia dominula*) (b) Gypsy Moth (*Lymantria dispar*) (c) Colorado Hawk Moth (*Euprosperpinus pinus weist*) (d) Silk Moth (*Bombyx mori*)

12

INSTITUTIONS AND ORGANIZATIONS

811. Which is the world's largest private international nature conservation organization with

3 million supporters and currently 27 affiliate and associate organizations on 5 continents?

(a) World Wide Fund for Nature (WWF)
(b) International Union of Conservation of Nature and Natural Resources (IUCN)
(c) Bombay Natural History Society (BNHS)
(d) Association for Conservation of Wildlife

812. In which year was the International Union for Conservation of Nature and Natural Resources founded?

(a) 1908 (b) 1928 (c) 1938 (d) 1948

813. Name an organization that monitors the status of ecosystems and species and plans conservation action for sustainable use of living resources in the world through its experts included in the six commissions:

(a) World Wide Fund for Nature (WWF)
(b) International Union for Conservation of Nature and Natural Resources (IUCN)
(c) Bombay Natural History Society (BNHS)
(d) Association for Conservation of Wildlife

814. Name the three most important United Nations agencies concerned with environmental conservation:

(a) FAO, UNESCO, UNEP (b) IUCN, FAO, UNEP (c) IUCN, FAO, UNEP (d) IUCN, WWF, ICBP

815. Name the U.N. agency responsible for execution of protected area management projects funded from U.N. sources such as United Nations Development Programme:

(a) United Nations Food and Agriculture Organization (FAO) (b) World Wild Fund for Nature (WWF) (c) International Union for

Conservation of Nature and Natural Resources (IUCN)

816. The United Nations Educational, Scientific and Cultural Organization operates through a Convention and a Man and Biosphere programme. Name the Convention:

(a) World Heritage Convention (b) Ramsar Convention (c) Bonn Convention (d) Whaling Convention

817. Name a United Nations agency which provides information service on environmental issues, holds conferences, produces publications and provides fellowships on conservation-related works:

(a) FAO (b) UNDP (c) IUCN (d) UNEP

818. Name the UNEP programme in the field of Protected Area Management:

(a) Regional Seas Programme (b) Programme on Desertification Problem (c) Global Environmental Monitoring System (GEMS) (d) All the above

819. Which agency or organization funded the turtle conservation in Irian Jaya, Indonesia?

(a) Organization of American States (b) European Economic Community (c) Council of Europe (d) World Wide Fund for Nature

820. Which agency funds the wildlife research in central America?

(a) Organization of American States (b) European Economic Community (c) Council of Europe (d) World Wide Fund for Nature

821. Which of the following is not a Non-Government Organization (NGO)?

(a) WWF (b) IUCN (c) FAO (d) All the above

822. By which international organization is the Commission on National Parks and Protected Areas (CNPPA) constituted?

(a) WWF (b) IUCN (c) FAO (d) EEC

823. In which year was the Commission on National Parks and Protected Areas established by IUCN?

(a) 1930 (b) 1940 (c) 1950 (d) 1960

824. Which international organization publishes the journal *Parks*?

(a) IUCN (b) WWF (c) BNHS (d) FAO

825. In which year was the Protected Area Data Unit at Cambridge established?

(a) 1961 (b) 1965 (c) 1970 (d) 1981

826. In which year was the first World Conference on National Parks in Seattle, Washington, held?

(a) 1932 (b) 1942 (c) 1952 (d) 1962

827. In which year was the second World Conference on National Park in Grand Teton Wyoming held?

(a) 1991 (b) 1985 (c) 1982 (d) 1972

828. Which city was the venue for International Conference on Marine Parks and Reserves 1975?

(a) Tokyo (b) New Delhi (c) Washington (d) Gland

829. Where are the headquarters of the World Wide Fund for Nature and International

Union for Conservation of Nature and Natural Resources located?

(a) Gland, Switzerland (b) Nairobi, Kenya (c) Paris, France (d) New Delhi, India

830. Where are the headquarters of the U.S. National Park Service located?

(a) Washington D.C. (b) San Fransisco (c) Paris (d) New York

831. Where are the United Nations Environment Programme (UNEP) headquarters located?

(a) Washington D.C. (b) Nairobi (c) Rome (d) New York

832. Where are the headquarters of the Food and Agriculture Organization (FAO) of the United Nations located?

(a) Washington D.C. (b) Nairobi (c) Rome (d) New York

833. Where are the headquarters of the National Audubon Society located?

(a) New York (b) London (c) Belgium (d) Washington D.C.

834. Where are the headquarters of the Center for International Environment Information situated?

(a) New York (b) London (c) Belgium (d) Washington D.C.

835. Which organization brings out the *Conservation News—Southeast Asia*?

(a) Association for the Conservation of Wildlife, Bangkok (b) International Centre of Conservation Education, England (c) Bombay Natural History Society, India (d) All the above

836. Name the wildlife newsletter being published by the FAO Regional Office for Asia and Far East, Bangkok, Thailand:

(a) *Silvicola* (b) *Tigerpaper* (c) *Silva* (d) *Myforest*

837. Where are the headquarters of the Elsa Wild Animal Appeal located?

(a) North Hollywood (b) Washington D.C. (c) New York (d) Nairobi

838. Which organization publishes the *African Wildlife News*?

(a) African Wildlife Foundation, Nairobi (b) East African Wildlife Society, Nairobi (c) Wildlife Conservation Society of Zambia, Lusaka (d) Food and Agriculture Organization

839. Which organization publishes the *Swara* magazine?

(a) African Wildlife Foundation, Nairobi (b) East African Wildlife Society, Nairobi (c) Wildlife Conservation Society of Zambia, Lusaka (d) Food and Agriculture Organization

840. Where is the Wildlife Institute of India located?

(a) Dehra Dun (b) Bombay (c) Bhopal (d) Udaipur

841. Where is the Indian Institute of Forest Management situated?

(a) Dehra Dun (b) Bombay (c) Bhopal (d) Udaipur

842. Where is the B.N.H.S. located?

(a) Dehra Dun (b) Bombay (c) Bhopal (d) Udaipur

843. Name the institution which imparts initial training in Forestry to the officers of the Indian Forest Service:

(a) Wildlife Institute of India, Dehra Dun (b) Indian Institute of Forest Management, Bhopal (c) Indira Gandhi National Forest Academy, Dehra Dun (d) State Forest Service College, Coimbatore

844. Where is the College of African Wildlife Management situated?

(a) Mweka, Tanzania (b) Nairobi, Kenya (c) Lusaka, Zambia (d) Accra, Ghana

845. Where is the School for Formation of Wildlife Specialists situated?

(a) Accra, Ghana (b) Garoua, Cameroon (c) Cairo, Egypt (d) Mweka, Tanzania

846. Where are the headquarters of the Caribbean Conservation Association located?

(a) Turrialba, Costa Rica (b) Barbados, West Indies (c) Lima, Peru (d) Mexico, Peru

847. Where are the headquarters of the International Waterfowl Research Bureau located?

(a) New Delhi (b) Slimbridge (c) London (d) Osaka

848. The World Commission on Environment and Development was chaired by Mrs. Gro Harlem Brundtland of Norway. In which year was it created?

(a) 1972 (b) 1978 (c) 1980 (d) 1983

CONVENTIONS AND INTERNATIONAL COOPERATION

849. Name the Convention which ensures support by the international community for world heritage sites?

(a) World Heritage Convention (b) Ramsar (c) Whaling Convention (d) CITES

850. The Convention concerning the protection of the World Cultural and Natural Heritage was adopted at the General Conference of the UNESCO on 15th November, 1972. When did it come into force?

(a) 17th December, 1972 (b) 17th December, 1975 (c) 17th December, 1974 (d) 17th December, 1991

851. The 'Convention of Wetlands of International Importance especially as Waterfowl Habitat' was signed on 2nd Feb., 1971, in an Iranian town and came into force on 21st December, 1985. Give the name by which the convention is popularly known:

(a) Bonn Convention (b) Ramsar Convention (c) Whaling Convention (d) World Heritage Convention

852. Which Convention was the first to aim for a worldwide participation and to concern itself exclusively with habitat?

(a) Bonn Convention (b) Ramsar Convention (c) Whaling Convention (d) World Heritage Convention

853. The 'Convention on the Conservation of Migratory Species of Wild Animals' was signed on 23rd June, 1979, and came into force on 1st November, 1983. What is the popular name of this Convention?

(a) Ramsar Convention (b) Bonn Convention (c) Whaling Convention (d) Bird Convention

854. The 'Convention on International Trade in Endangered Species of Wild Fauna and Flora' (CITES) was adopted in 1973. When did it come into force?

(a) 1972 (b) 1973 (c) 1974 (d) 1975

855. How many appendices does the CITES include?

(a) 2 (b) 3 (c) 4 (d) 5

856. What is the content of the appendices of the CITES?

(a) List of endangered species of plants
(b) List of endangered species of animals
(c) List of endangered species of plants and animals (d) List of endangered habitats

857. Under the 'World Heritage Convention' which agency assists in technical matters related to the management of *natural sites*?

(a) IUCN (b) ICOMOS (c) WWF (d) FAO

858. Under the 'World Heritage Convention' which agency provides the technical guidance related to the management of *cultural sites*?

(a) International Council for Monuments and Sites (b) I.U.C.N. (c) U.N.E.P. (d) All the above

859. In which year was the World Charter for Nature adopted by the U.N. General Assembly?

(a) October 29, 1981 (b) October 29, 1980 (c) October 29, 1982 (d) October 29, 1991

860. In the year 1958 between Feb. 3 and 8, representatives of twelve Asian countries got together in India and formulated an Action Plan for the Protected Areas of Indo-Malayan Realm. What is the popular name of this Action Plan?

(a) Asian Action Plan (b) Bali Action Plan (c) Wildlife Plan (d) Corbett Action Plan

861. Which country was the venue for the launch of the World Conservation Strategy?

(a) Uganda (b) Nepal (c) Bhutan (d) India

862. What kind of habitats are listed in *Ramsar List?*

(a) Rainforests (b) Wetlands (c) Deserts (d) All the above

863. What kind of habitat is likely to be a *Ramsar Site?*

(a) Wetland (b) Boreal Forest (c) Deserts (d) All the above

864. In which year was the African Convention on the Conservation of Nature and Natural Resources adopted?

(a) 1938 (b) 1948 (c) 1958 (d) 1968

865. What is the aim of the African Convention on the Conservation of Nature and Natural Resources?

(a) Control in trade of species and its products (b) Establishing the agencies for implementation of convention (c) Conservation education (d) All the above

866. In which year was the Convention on Nature Protection and Wildlife Preservation in the Western Hemisphere adopted?
(a) 1980 (b) 1970 (c) 1950 (d) 1940

867. In which year was the Convention on Conservation of Nature in the South Pacific adopted?
(a) 1971 (b) 1976 (c) 1989 (d) 1991

868. In which year was the Convention for the Conservation of Vicuna signed?
(a) 1969 (b) 1982 (c) 1990 (d) 1991

869. Name the countries which are party to the Vicuna Convention:
(a) India, Nepal and Pakistan (b) USSR, USA and UK (c) Argentina, Bolivia, Chili, Ecuador and Peru (d) All the above

870. What kind of species of plants and animals are listed in Appendix I of the Convention on International Trade in Endangered Species of Wild Fauna and Flora (CITES)?
(a) All species threatened with extinction, which are or may be affected by trade (b) All species which could become endangered unless trade is controlled (c) Any species other than already listed in Appendix I & II, on which any CITES party wants to regulate the international trade (d) All the above

871. What kind of plant and animal species are listed in Appendix II of the CITES?

(a) All species which could become en-dangered unless trade is controlled (b) Any species other than already listed in Appendix I & II on which any CITES party wants to regulate the international trade (c) All species threatened with extinction, which are or may be affected by trade (d) All the above

872. What kind of plant and animal species are listed in Appendix III of the CITES?

(a) All species threatened with extinction, which are or may be affected by trade (b) All species which could become endangered unless trade is controlled. (c) Any species other than already listed in Appendix I & II, on which any CITES party wants to regulate the international trade (d) All the above

873. Who is responsible for the enforcement of the provisions of the CITES?

(a) United Nations (b) Member States (c) FAO (d) WWF

874. Where is the CITES Secretariat located?

(a) India (b) Switzerland (c) USA (d) Kenya

875. Which country launched *Operation Bicornis* to save the Black Rhino from extinction?

(a) Namibia (b) Zimbabwe (c) Zambia (d) India

876. Which country launched *Operation Stronghold* to save the Black Rhino from extinction?

(a) Namibia (b) Zimbabwe (c) Zambia (d) India

877. In which year was the International Polar Bear Agreement signed among the 5 circum-

polar nations to protect the Polar Bear (*Thalarctos maritimus*) and its habitat?
(a) 1960 (b) 1975 (c) 1990 (d) 1991

878. In which year was the Wildlife and Countryside Act passed in the United Kingdom?
(a) 1979 (b) 1980 (c) 1983 (d) 1981

NATIONAL PARKS AND PROTECTED AREAS

879. What is nature conservation in modern sense?
(a) Sustainable maintenance and utilization of earth's resources (b) Total ban on economic exploitation of resources (c) Establishment of National Parks and Protected Areas (d) All the above

880. Based upon the objectives of the protected areas IUCN has given a classification. How many categories of protected areas are recognized as per 1984 classification?
(a) 3 (b) 5 (c) 8 (d) 10

881. *Strict Nature Reserve* or *Scientific Reserve* are meant to conserve ecologically representative examples of nature. Which one of the following protected areas fall under this category?
(a) Yala Strict Reserve, Sri Lanka (b) Barro Colorado Island, Panama (c) Gombe Stream National Park, Tanzania (d) All the above

882. National Parks are meant to protect the areas of national or international significance for recreation, scientific and education use. Which of the following fall under this category?

(a) Corbett National Park, India (b) Bandhavgarh National Park, India (c) Etosha National Park, Namibia (d) All the above

883. *National Monument* and *National Landmark* are meant to protect the unique natural features of national significance. Which of the following areas fall under this category?

(a) Angkor Wat National Park, Kampuchea (b) Petrified Forests Nature Monument, Argentina (c) Gedi National Monument, Kenya (d) All the above

884. *Wildlife Sanctuary* or *Managed Nature Reserve* are meant to protect the natural conditions essential for the species, group of species or physical environment. Limited forestry operations and resource harvest is permitted. Which of the following protected areas fall under this category?

(a) Dandeli Wildlife Sanctuary, India (b) Bori Wildlife Sanctuary, India (c) Both above (d) None

885. *Protected Landscape and Seascape* are meant to maintain the areas of national significance where man and land interaction is permitted and traditional land uses are continued. Which one of the following areas fall under this category?

(a) Pululahua Geobotanical Reserve, Ecuador
(b) Machu Ricchu Historic Sanctuary, Peru
(c) Both the above (d) None

886. *Resource reserves* are areas yet to be classified as a permanent protected area and once objectives are defined it is to be put to appropriate category. Which of the following areas come under this category?
(a) South Turkana National Reserve, Kenya
(b) Tahuamanu Protected Forest, Bolivia
(c) Both the above (d) None

887. *Multiple Use Management Area* and *Managed Resource Areas* are meant for sustained yield of water, wood, wildlife, pasture and tourism. Which of the following areas fall under this category?
(a) Ngorongoro Conservation Area, Tanzania
(b) Kutai National Park, Indonesia (c) Jamari National Forest, Brazil (d) All the above

888. *Biosphere Reserve* is any protected area so declared in order to conserve flora and fauna, and to safeguard the genetic diversity of species. Which of the following protected areas are biosphere reserves?
(a) Nilgiri Biosphere Reserve, India (b) Sinharaja Forest Reserve, Sri Lanka (c) Both the above (d) Keoladeo National Park, India

889. *World Heritage Sites* are meant to protect the natural features of universal significance and are nominated under the World Heritage Convention. Which of the following protected areas is a World Heritage Site?

(a) Serengati National Park, Tanzania
(b) Keoladeo National Park, India (c) Darien
National Park, Panama (d) All the above

890. Which country has adopted nomenclature of
National Park, Sanctuaries, Game Reserve and
Closed Areas for the various categories of its
protected areas under its Wildlife Protection
Act?

(a) India (b) Panama (c) England (d) Kenya

891. 'There are floating islands on lakes in
Kashmir, Burma and North America that I
have heard of but I think that... this... is the
only floating wildlife sanctuary in the world.'
Thus wrote E.P. Gee in his book *The Wildlife
of India*. Which Protected Area is he referring
to?

(a) Dachigam National Park (b) Periyar Tiger
Reserve (c) Keibul Lamjao National Park
(d) Kanha National Park

892. Which is the last refuge of the Asiatic lion
(*Panthera leo persica*) in the wild?

(a) Kaziranga National Park (b) Gir National
Park (c) Periyar National Park (d) Kanha
National Park

893. Which tiger reserve forms a linking corridor
for Asiatic Elephant (*Elephas maximus*) migration between the forests of Bhutan and Manas
Tiger Reserve in Assam, India?

(a) Kaziranga (b) Buxa (c) Namdapha
(d) Indravati

894. A wetland in India included in the World
Heritage Site (natural) was created by a
Maharaja as a shooting preserve for wildfowls.

It now serves as the winter refuge for Siberian Crane (*Grus leucogeranus*). Name it:

(a) Keoladeo Ghana (b) Rangathittu (c) Chilka (d) Nelapattu

895. In the year 1979 an area in Nepal was declared a World Heritage Site. It comprises Everest, Choster and Chooyu peaks of Nepal. Name this protected area:

(a) Sagarmatha National Park (b) Lake Rara National Park (c) Royal Chitwan National Park (d) All the above

896. Which protected area is called the N'-Gorongoro of India?

(a) Kanha National Park (b) Bandhavgarh National Park (c) Panna National Park (d) Sariska Tiger Reserve

897. Which tiger reserve in India holds as many as twenty species of fauna listed in the IUCN Red Date Book?

(a) Kanha Tiger Reserve (b) Bandhavgarh National Park (c) Manas Tiger Reserve (d) Ranthambhore Tiger Reserve

898. Name the largest nesting site of the greater flamingo (*Phoenicopterus reseus*) in Asia:

(a) Little Rann of Kutch (b) Great Rann of Kutch (c) Both the above (d) None of the above

899. Selection of sites for national parks and protected areas could be based on species or ecosystems. What approach was followed in the selection of sites for tiger reserves established under the Project Tiger?

(a) Tiger (*Panthera tigris*) taken as a key species (b) All representative ecosystems of Tiger's range were selected (c) Both the above (d) None

900. What do you mean by *In Situ Genebanks?*

(a) Protected areas and natural ecosystem containing wild gene pools of actual or potential economic importance (b) Seeds of a species deposited in the seed-banks (c) Both the above (d) None of the above

901. What approach was followed in Brazil to select the sites for National Park and Protected Areas?

(a) Selection of areas with many plant communities (b) Pleistocene Refugia (c) Both the above (d) Not known

902. Transfrontier reservess of two or more countries provide a larger protected area unit. Name the countries involved in Ruwenzori-Virunga Volcanoes System?

(a) Uganda, Rwanda and Zaire (b) Uganda, Zaire and Egypt (c) Zaire, Kenya and Somalia (d) Kenya, Somalia, Uganda

903. Name the protected area neighbouring Serengati National Park of Tanzania:

(a) Masai Mara, National Reserve, Kenya
(b) Tindu Reserve, Papua New Guinea
(c) Mkomazi Game Reserve, Tanzania
(d) Mana Pools National Park, Zimbabwe

904. Name the protected area neighbouring Wassur Game Reserve of Indonesia:

(a) Masai Mara, National Reserve, Kenya
(b) Tindu Reserve, Papua New Guinea
(c) Mkomazi Game Reserve, Tanzania (d) Lag Badana National Park, Somalia

905. Name the protected area neighbouring Tsavo National Park of Kenya:

(a) Masai Mara, National Reserve, Kenya
(b) Tindu Reserve, Papua New Guinea
(c) Mkomazi Game Reserve, Tanzania
(d) Gemsbok National Park, Botswana

906. Name the protected area that shares the boundaries with Lower Zambezi National Park of Zambia:

(a) Mana Pools National Park, Zimbabwe (b) Iguacu National Park, Brazil (c) Cerro Sajama National Park, Bolivia (d) Lag Badana National Park, Somalia

907. Name the protected area sharing boundaries with Iguazu National Park of Argentina:

(a) Mana Pools National Park, Zimbabwe (b) Iguacu National Park, Brazil (c) Cerro Sajama National Park, Bolivia (d) Lag Badana National Park, Somalia

908. Name the protected area sharing boundaries with Lauca National Park of Chile:

(a) Mana Pools National Park, Zimbabwe (b) Iguacu National Park, Brazil (c) Cerro Sajama National Park, Bolivia (d) Lag Badana National Park, Somalia

909. Name the protected area sharing boundaries with Yot Dom Wildlife Sanctuary of Thailand:

(a) Lag Badana National Park, Somalia
(b) Gemsbok National Park, Botswana
(c) Preh Vihea, Kampuchea (d) Iguacu National Park, Brazil

910. Which protected area shares boundaries with Boni National Park of Kenya?

(a) Preh Vihea, Kampuchea (b) Lag Badana National Park, Somalia (c) Gemsbok National Park, Botswana (d) Iguacu National Park, Brazil

911. Which protected area shares boundaries with Kalahari Gemsbok National Park of South Africa?

(a) Preh Vihea, Kampuchea (b) Lag Badana National Park, Somalia (c) Gemsbok National Park, Botswana (d) Iguacu National Park, Brazil

912. Name the countries sharing boundaries of Manas Wildlife Sanctuary:

(a) India and Bhutan (b) Costa Rica and Panama (c) India and Bangladesh (d) Bhutan and Nepal

913. Name the countries sharing boundaries of La Amisted Reserve:

(a) India and Bhutan (b) Costa Rica and Panama (c) India and Bangladesh (d) Bhutan and Nepal

914. Name the countries sharing boundaries of Sundarbans National Park:

(a) India and Bhutan (b) Costa Rica and Panama (c) India and Bangladesh (d) Bhutan and Nepal

915. Name the countries sharing boundaries of Mount Nimba Strict Nature Reserve:

(a) Guinea and Ivory Coast (b) Malawi and Zambia (c) Bhutan and India (d) Nepal and Bhutan

916. Name the countries sharing boundaries of Nyika National Park:

(a) Guinea and Ivory Coast (b) Malawi and Zambia (c) Bhutan and India (d) Nepal and Bhutan

917. Yadua Taba Island in Fiji was under the traditional ownership of Matagali natives. It is a habitat of Crested Iguana. Threats to habitat were posed from goat grazing and slash and burn agriculture. What management strategy is followed to protect Crested Iguana?

(a) Appointment of natives as honorary wardens (b) Payment of compensation to natives for non-grazing by goats (c) Ban on shifting cultivation (d) All above

918. In which country is *Foundation para Parques Nacionalis*, a foundation for national park system, located?

(a) Panama (b) Costa Rica (c) India (d) All the above

919. Guatemala has a unique system of protected area management. What is it?

(a) University of San Carlos selects nature reserves called *Biotopes* (b) Non-government organizations manage the *Biotopes* (c) Both the above

920. Name the non-governmental organization responsible for establishment, management and development of protected areas in Belize:

(a) Belize Audubon Society (b) Belize — WWF (c) Belize — IUCN (d) All the above

921. If we want to involve the native tribal populations in management of protected areas for conservation and traditional sustainable use of natural resources, in which management category should the area be classified?

(a) World Heritage Site (b) Biosphere Reserve (c) National Park (d) Wildlife Sanctuary

922. Mapimi Reserve protects an endangered species of tortoise with the help of local people. In which country is it located?

(a) Panama (b) Honduras (c) Mexico (d) India

923. How national parks and protected areas contribute to socio-economic development?

(a) Conservation of renewable resources, soil and water (b) Protection of genetic resources breeding stock and bio-diversity (c) Eco-development, tourism, and preservation of cultural traditions of the local people (d) All the above

924. Due to construction of Kariba Dam in the river Zambezi change in water flow below the dam has caused bank erosion and resulted in the shallower and wider stream in a National Park of Zimbabwe. Name this park:

(a) Mana Pool National Park (b) Chirisa Safari Area (c) Gonare Zhou National Park (d) Guatapo National Park

925. Guatapo National Park protects the catchment areas of four dams. It is an important source of drinking water for the capital city of the country which you have to name:

(a) England (b) Botswana (c) Venezuela (d) Pakistan

926. Name the National Park in Venezuela which includes the world-famous Angel Falls:

(a) Guatapo National Park (b) Canaima National Park (c) Yapacana National Park (d) Mana Pool National Park

927. Name the Protected Area in Venezuela that serves as the source of water for the Caroni River System on which major hydroelectric project is being constructed:

(a) Canaima National Park (b) Guatapo National Park (c) Yapacana National Park (d) All the above

928. What should be reasonably beneficial logging practice to the wildlife in the multiple use forests?

(a) Leaving unworked natural forest patches interspersed with logged areas (b) Trees yielding non-wood forest produce should not be felled (c) Fire protection (d) All the above

929. Protected Areas in India may serve the vital function of sustained yield of economic and locally harvested natural resource. What function is performed by protected mangroves?

(a) Protection to fish spawning (b) Protection to prawn production (c) Protection to nesting birds (d) All the above

930. Properly managed protected areas can provide sustained yield of animal resources for economic development. Name the country where capybara farms exist:

(a) India (b) Venezuela (c) Switzerland (d) All the above

931. Which of the following species hold the potential for raw material supply to the leather industry through farming?

(a) Crocodiles (b) Snakes (c) Deer (d) All the above

932. In New Guinea rare Birdwing Butterflies (*Ornithoptera*) farming is done by villagers by growing *Aristolochia* vines in the gardens to attract females from nearby forests to lay eggs in the gardens. Villagers protect caterpillars against predation and collect pupae. Hatching adults are killed and sold in the market. What is the benefit of this project?

(a) Wild stock is not collected as specimens are available at low price (b) Caterpillars which remain uncollected rebuild the wild stock (c) Economic gains to rural poor (d) All the above

933. Conservation and economic yield can be combined with the help of wildlife farming for the species rendered endangered by trade. Name the country that carries out farming of Rusa deer, Wallabies, Megapodes, Cassowary, Crocodile and Birdwing Butterfly to rebuild the wild stock as well as sell it for economic yield:

(a) Papua New Guinea (b) Panama (c) India (d) Mexico

934. What is a 'Buffer Zone' in the protected area management?

(a) Area around or adjacent to protected area where land use favours the public needs (b) Protective surroundings of nature reserve to minimise conflict between people and wildlife (c) Both the above (d) None

935. Which group of native people are assisting park managers in the Sagarmatha National Park in Nepal?

(a) Rana (b) Sherpa (c) Jarwa (d) Kol

936. What is the management strategy of Kuna Yala Reserve in Panama?

(a) Local tribals, Kuna, established the park to protect natural and cultural resources (b) Assistance in planning and training to Kuna Yala for technical self-sufficiency in park management (c) Resource mobilization through tourism (d) All the above

937. What is the benefit of a Multiple Use Wetland?

(a) Protection to aquatic flora and fauna and wildfowl (b) Economic yield to people through fisheries (c) Ground water recharge (d) All the above

938. What is the gene erosion?

(a) Death of a plant or animal without reproduction (b) Irretrievable loss of populations (c) Both the above (d) None

939. What habitat management strategy is advised by Asad R. Rahmania, scientist at Bombay Natural History Society, to protect the Bustards and Floricans in India?

(a) Protection of open forests (b) Protection of wetlands (c) Protection of grasslands (d) Protection of rain forests

940. Name the primate protected in the Virunga Volcanoes National Park:

(a) Chimpanzee (*Pan troglodytes*) (b) Liontailed Macaque (*Macaca silenus*) (c) Gorilla (*Gorilla gorilla*) (d) All the above

941. What information is required to manage the rare and endangered animals?

(a) Population dynamics (b) Habitat requirements (c) Causes of decline (d) All the above

942. In the wildfires of the year 1985 in Galapagos Island National Park tortoises were threatened with local extinction. What strategy was adopted to manage the crisis?

(a) Airlifting and shifting of tortoises to safety and then fire-fighting (b) Fire-fighting with helicopters without airlifting tortoises (c) The situation was left to nature (d) All the above

943. What measure should be adopted to help declining population of turtles from egg predation?

(a) Killing all predators (b) Fencing the turtle nest-site to prevent predation by lizards and pigs (c) Keeping them in zoo (d) Not known

944. If an animal species threatened with extinction is unable to recover even after habitat loss has been stopped, migration corridors have been provided, predation level reduced, welfare factors provided, exotic and feral animals eliminated, diseases controlled and habitat suitably manipulated, what should be the last resort to save the species from extinction?

(a) Captive breeding and release in suitable habitats (b) Identification and elimination of the cause of threat (c) Both the above (d) The species cannot be saved

945. What was the management strategy followed to save the Kakapo, ground-living parrot of New Zealand and Kri Kri Ibex from extinction?

(a) Capture of animals from mainland and release in the islands where predators and competitors are absent (b) Captive breeding and release in the wild (c) Protection of the original habitat in mainland (d) All the above

946. If wild animals of a species have become overabundant in a protected area, what should be the management strategy?

(a) Providing dispersal corridors of protected habitat (b) Capture and translocation to other suitable habitats (c) Culling of some individuals (d) All the above

947. What is the usual practice applied to manage the locally overabundant populations of threatened African Elephant (*Locodonta africana*) in some protected areas of Africa?

(a) Capture and relocation to other suitable habitats (b) Culling (i.e. selective killing) (c) Introduction of predators (d) All the above

948. Which protected area is the last refuge of endemic bird Bali Starling?

(a) Kutai National Park (b) Bali Barat National Park (c) Araguaia National Park (d) Manu National Park

949. Which was the first designated national park of Kenya?

(a) Saiwa Swamp National Park (b) Nairobi National Park (c) Lake Nakuru National Park (d) Mt. Kenya National Park

950. Name a national park in Kenya famous for perpetual snow on the equator of the earth:

(a) Mt. Kenya National Park (b) Mt. Elgon National Park (c) Dodori National Park (d) Shimba Hills National Park

951. Joy Adamson's book *Born Free* made famous a national park of Kenya. Name it:

(a) Meru National Park (b) Kora National Park (c) Both the above (d) Saiwa Swapo National Park

952. Lake Bogoria National Reserve in Kenya was designated to protect a specific animal. Name it:

(a) Greater Kudu (*Tragelaphus strepsiceros*) (b) Impala (*Aepyceros melampus*) (c) Olive Baboon (*Papio cynocephalus*) (d) Puku (*Adenota vardonii*)

953. Name the smallest national park in Kenya created to protect the Sitatunga Antelope and Brazza's Monkey:

(a) Saiwa Swamp National Park (b) Limbwe Valley National Park (c) Mount Elgon National Park (d) Kakamega Forest National Reserve

954. Based on the study in a national park of Kenya Cynthia Moss and her colleagues wrote a book, *Elephant Memories*. Name the park:

(a) Sibiloi National Park (b) Amboseli National Park (c) Kora National Park (d) Kariandus National Park

955. In which national park of Kenya are the famous Mzima Springs, which gush out 50 million gallons of water every day, situated?

(a) Tsavo West National Park (b) Ruma National Park (c) Massai Mara National Park (d) Meru National Park

956. Colonel Patterson wrote a book, *The Maneaters of Tsavo*, telling the story of the marauding animals playing havoc on the labours engaged to construct the Mombasa-Nairobi railway line. Which animal was described in the book?

(a) Leopard (*Panthera pardus*) (b) Cheetah (*Acinonyx jubatus*) (c) Lion (*Panthera leo*) (d) Hunting Dog (*Lycaon pictus*)

957. In which national park of Kenya, River Galana forms the spectacular Lugard Falls?

(a) Tsavo East National Park (b) Aberdare National Park (c) Longonot National Park (d) Bisandi National Park

958. Name a national park in Kenya that was created to protect the Roan Antelope (*Hippotragus equinus*):

(a) Shimba Hills National Park (b) Kakamega Forest National Reserve (c) Saiwa National Park (d) Lambwe Valley National Park

959. Incredibly beautiful Serengeti National Park is the largest and the oldest national park of Tanzania covering an area of over 14,500 square kilometres. In which year was it established?

(a) 1901 (b) 1945 (c) 1951 (d) 1961

960. Based on the studies at Serengeti National Park a famous book and movie was produced, *Serengeti Shall Not Die*. Who wrote the book?

(a) Bernard Grizmek and Michael Grizmek (b) Kailash Sankhala (c) Fateh Singh Rathore (d) Deborah Appleton

961. Name the National Park of Tanzania which has the highest peak in Africa (5,895 m):

(a) Ngorongoro Conservation Area (b) Selous Game Reserve (c) Kilimanjaro National Park (d) Ruaha National Park

962. Which is the largest Protected Area in Africa?

(a) Serengeti National Park (b) Kilimanjaro National Park (c) Lake Manyara National Park (d) Selous Game Reserve

963. Name the national park in Tanzania established primarily to protect the chimpanzee (*Pan troglodytes*):

(a) Gombe National Park (b) Mahale Mountains National Park (c) Both the above (d) Arusha National Park

964. Unlike leopards, lions are ground dwelling cats seldom taking to trees. However there are two national parks containing the exceptional tree-climbing lions in the world. Name these parks:

(a) Lake Manyara National Park, Tanzania (b) Queen Elizabeth National Park, Uganda (c) Gir National Park, India (d) Both (a) and (b) (e) Both (b) and (c)

965. Which is the largest national park of Uganda?

(a) Queen Elizabeth National Park (b) Lake Mburo National Park (c) Kidepo Valley National Park (d) Murchison Falls National Park

966. In which country are the Awash National Park and Bale Mountain National Park situated?

(a) England (b) Uganda (c) Ethiopia (d) Nepal

967. Which national park of Ethiopia sustains the maximum concentration of endemic Mountain Nyala (*Tragelaphus buxtoni*) in the world?

(a) Nechisar National Park (b) Bale Mountains National Park (c) Awash National Park (d) Abijatta Shalla Lakes National Park

968. Largest National Park of Rwanda spreads over an area of 2,500 square kilometres and is the home of over 500 species of birds. Name this park:

(a) Lake Kivu (b) Forest Naturelle de Nyungwe (c) Park National des Volcans (d) Akagera National Park

969. Which is the oldest designated national park in Africa?

(a) Parc National des Volcans, Rwanda (b) Bale Mountain National Park, Ethiopia (c) Nairobi National Park, Kenya (d) Kilimanjaro National Park, Tanzania

970. Dian Fossey wrote the book *Gorillas in the Mist* based on her study in a national park of several years. Name the national park where she was murdered in the year 1985:

(a) Parc National des Volcans, Rwanda (b) Bale Mountain National Park, Ethiopia (c) Nairobi National Park, Kenya (d) Kilimanjaro National Park, Tanzania

971. In which country is the Guatapo National Park located?

(a) Venezuela (b) Zaire (c) USA (d) Somalia

972. In which country is the Garamba National Park, the last home of Northern White Rhino, located?

(a) Venezuela (b) Zaire (c) USA (d) Somalia

973. In which country is the Everglades National Park located?

(a) Venezuela (b) Zaire (c) USA (d) Somalia

974. In which country is the Jaru Biological Reserve located?

(a) Canada (b) Panama (c) Argentina (d) Brazil

975. In which country is the Kuna Yala Reserve located?

(a) Canada (b) Panama (c) Argentina (d) Brazil

976. In which country is the Lanin National Park located?

(a) Canada (b) Panama (c) Argentina (d) Brazil

977. In which country is the Ngorongoro Conservation Area located?

(a) Peru (b) India (c) Canada (d) Tanzania

978. In which country is the Kanha and Ranthambhore Tiger Reserve located?

(a) Peru (b) India (c) Canada (d) Tanzania

979. Which is the first designated national park in the world?

(a) Corbett National Park, India (b) Yellowstone National Park, USA (c) Lanin National Park, Argentina (d) Not known

980. Which national park is included in the IUCN list of the world's most threatened protected areas on account of acid rain pollution?

(a) Krkonose National Park, Czechoslovakia (b) Manu National Park, Peru (c) Kutai National Park, Indonesia (d) Bali Barat National Park, Indonesia

981. In which country is Boni National Reserve located?

(a) Kenya (b) Botswana (c) Ivory Coast (d) Kampuchea

982. In which country is the Central Kalahari Game Reserve located?

(a) Kenya (b) Botswana (c) Ivory Coast (d) Kampuchea

983. In which country is the Comoe National Park located?

(a) Kenya (b) Botswana (c) Ivory Coast (d) Kampuchea

984. In which country is the Angkor Wat National Park located?

(a) Kenya (b) Botswana (c) Ivory Coast (d) Kampuchea

985. Which habitat is the last refuge of the echo parakeet (*Psittacula echo*)?

(a) Black River Gorge, Mauritius (b) Tamang Neggara National Park, Malaya (c) Tung Yai Reserve, Thailand (d) Mengyan Reserve, China

986. In which country is the Sikhote Alin Reserve situated?

(a) USSR (b) UK (c) USA (d) China

987. In which country is the Salak Pra Reserve located?

(a) UK (b) USSR (c) USA (d) Thailand

988. In which country is the Huai Kha Khaeng Reserve located?

(a) UK (b) USSR (c) USA (d) Thailand

989. In which country is the Tung Yai Reserve located?

(a) UK (b) USSR (c) USA (d) Thailand

990. The world's first white tiger safari was inaugurated on October 1, 1991. Where is it located?

(a) Nandan Kanan, Bhubaneswar, Orissa
(b) Pendari Kanan, Bilaspur (c) Narohill,
Satna, Madhya Pradesh (d) Hyderabad,
Andhra Pradesh

15
PHOTO QUIZ

991. Identify this animal photographed in a
national park in Africa:

(a) Burchell's Zebra (*Equus burchelli*)
(b) Grevy's Zebra (*Equus grevyi*) (c) Common
Giraffe (*Giraffa camelopardalis*) (d) Reticulated
Giraffe (*Giraffa reticulatus*)

992. The cat photographed here is found
thoughout south-east Asia but not in Sri
Lanka. It looks like a miniature replica of
the leopard found in Asia and Africa. Name
the cat:

(a) Leopard cat (b) Fishing cat (c) Slow Loris
(d) Slender Loris

993. Identify the species shown here. It is a
nocturnal primate found in north-east India:

(a) Slender Loris (*Loris tardigradus*) (b) Slow
Loris (*Nycticebus coucany*) (c) Rhesus Macaque
(*Macaca mulatta*) (d) Bonnet Macaque (*Macaca
radiata*)

994. Identify this animal, in Hindu mythology
known as the monkey-god Hanuman who
helped Lord Rama to conquer King Ravana:

(a) Nilgiri Langur (*Presbytis johnii*) (b) Common Langur (*Presbytis entellus*) (c) Golden

Langur *(Presbytis geei)* (d) Capped Langur
(Presbytis pileatus)

995. The crane depicted here breeds in central
Asia, Mongolia, Crimea and the Ukraine.
During winters it migrates southwards to
Africa and the Indian subcontinent. Identify
the species:

(a) Sarus Crane *(Grus antigone)* (b) Siberian
Crane *(Grus leucogeranus)* (c) Demoiselle Crane
(Anthropoides virgo) (d) Common Crane *(Grus
grus)*

996. Sir Martin Ewans commented in his book,
Bharatpur: Bird Paradise, about the crane
shown here: 'This crane is a cynosure of
Bharatpur.' It is a regular winter visitor to
India from its breeding grounds in north-
eastern Yakutia, between the Yana and Kelyne
and the Ob rivers. Identify this crane:

(a) Sarus Crane *(Grus antigone)* (b) Siberian
Crane *(Grus leucogeranus)* (c) Demoiselle Crane
(Anthropoides virgo) (d) Common Crane *(Grus
grus)*

997. Identify the bird with the peculiar bill and
prominent crest depicted in the photograph.
It is found in Egypt, central and southern
Asia, China, India and Japan:

(a) Spoonbill *(Platalea leucordia)* (b) White Ibis
'Threskiornis melanocephala) (c) Glossy Ibis
(Plegadis falcinellus) (d) Great White Egret
(Egretta alba)

998. Birds of prey feed mainly on small rodents
and other birds. Identify the bird
photographed here with its prey:

(a) Goshawk *(Accipiter gentilis)* (b) Sparrow-hawk *(Accipiter nisus)* (c) Bonelli's Hawk-Eagle *(Hieraaetus fasciatus)* (d) Shikra *(Accipiter badius)*

999. An Eurasian bird of prey was exterminated in many north European countries, mainly because of shooting. Recently some of this species have been re-established in Sweden where the last bird was sighted in 1950. Identify the species shown in the photograph:

(a) Little Owl *(Athene noctua)* (b) Eagle Owl *(Bubo bubo)* (c) Laughing Owl *(Scelogglaux albifacies)* (d) Tawny Owl *(Strix aluco)*

1000. People of the Kol tribe in central India use the root tubers of the plant shown here as oral ethnomedicine against snake-bites. Identify the plant which occurs in Africa where it is known as 'the flame lily':

(a) Flame of the Forests or *Palas (Butea monosperma)* (b) Flame of the Deserts or *Rohira (Tecomella undulata)* (c) Orange-bell Lily *(Lilium grayii)* (d) Tiger Lily *(Gloriosa superba)*

991

992

993

994

995

996

997

998

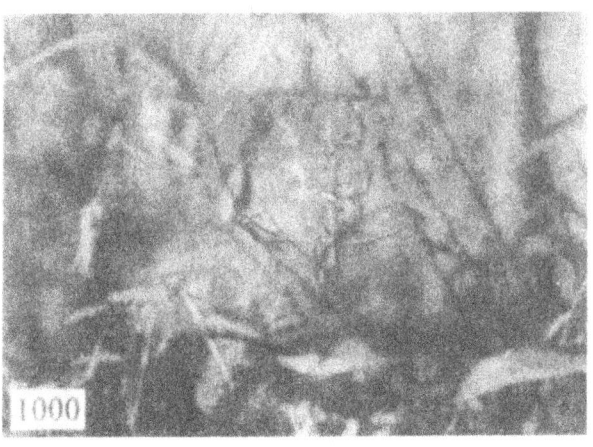

1000

999

ANSWERS

CHAPTER 1

1. (a)	2. (a)	3. (b)	4. (a)	5. (a)	6. (b)
7. (c)	8. (a)	9. (b)	10. (a)	11. (b)	12. (d)
13. (a)	14. (b)	15. (b)	16. (a)	17. (c)	18 (b)
19. (d)	20. (a)	21. (b)	22. (b)	23. (c)	24. (a)
25. (b)	26. (a)	27. (b)	28. (b)	29. (d)	30. (b)

CHAPTER 2

31. (a)	32. (b)	33. (c)	34. (c)	35. (b)	36. (c)
37. (d)	38. (a)	39. (b)	40. (c)	41. (a)	42. (b)
43. (c)	44. (d)	45. (a)	46. (a)	47. (a)	48. (a)
49. (b)	50. (a)	51. (b)	52. (a)	53. (a)	54. (a)
55. (a)	56. (b)	57. (b)	58. (a)	59. (b)	60. (a)

CHAPTER 3

61. (a)	62. (a)	63. (b)	64. (c)	65. (a)	66. (b)
67. (a)	68. (a)	69. (c)	70. (b)	71. (c)	72. (a)
73. (a)	74. (a)	75. (b)	76. (c)	77. (a)	78. (c)
79. (b)	80. (d)	81. (a)	82. (b)	83. (c)	84. (a)
85. (b)	86. (c)	87. (a)	88. (b)	89. (c)	90. (d)
91. (a)	92. (b)	93. (c)	94. (a)	95. (b)	96. (c)
97. (a)	98. (b)	99. (c)	100. (a)	101. (b)	102. (c)
103. (a)	104. (a)	105. (a)	106. (c)	107. (a)	108. (a)
109. (b)	110. (a)	111. (a)	112. (c)	113. (a)	114. (b)
115. (c)	116. (a)	117. (d)	118. (d)	119. (c)	120. (d)
121. (a)	122. (a)	123. (b)	124. (a)	125. (b)	126. (b)
127. (a)	128. (b)	129. (b)	130. (a)	131. (a)	132. (b)
133. (c)	134. (c)	135. (a)	136. (c)	137. (b)	138. (a)
139. (a)	140. (a)	141. (c)	142. (d)	143. (b)	144. (a)
145. (b)	146. (c)				

CHAPTER 4

147. (a)	148. (a)	149. (a)	150. (d)	151. (a)	152. (d)
153. (b)	154. (d)	155. (b)	156. (b)	157. (a)	158. (c)
159. (c)	160. (b)	161. (a)	162. (b)	163. (a)	164. (c)
165. (b)	166. (a)	167. (b)	168. (a)	169. (a)	170. (a)
171. (c)	172. (c)	173. (b)	174. (b)	175. (c)	176. (b)
177. (a)	178. (a)	179. (c)	180. (b)	181. (a)	182. (d)
183. (c)	184. (a)	185. (a)	186. (d)	187. (b)	188. (c)
189. (d)	190. (a)	191. (a)	192. (a)	193. (a)	194. (a)
195. (a)	196. (a)	197. (a)	198. (b)	199. (b)	200. (a)
201. (b)	202. (d)	203. (d)	204. (d)	205. (a)	206. (b)
207. (c)	208. (a)	209. (b)	210. (c)	211. (d)	212. (d)

CHAPTER 5

213. (c)	214. (a)	215. (d)	216. (d)	217. (d)	218. (d)
219. (a)	220. (d)	221. (c)	222. (a)	223. (b)	224. (a)
225. (b)	226. (b)	227. (b)	228. (d)	229. (a)	230. (a)
231. (c)	232. (b)	233. (b)	234. (a)	235. (b)	236. (c)
237. (a)	238. (b)	239. (c)	240. (d)	241. (c)	242. (a)
243. (c)	244. (b)	245. (a)	246. (a)	247. (a)	248. (d)
249. (a)					

CHAPTER 6

250. (d)	251. (d)	252. (a)	253. (d)	254. (b)	255. (c)
256. (c)	257. (a)	258. (c)	259. (d)	260. (a)	261. (b)
262. (a)	263. (d)	264. (b)	265. (a)	266. (b)	267. (a)
268. (a)	269. (c)	270. (d)	271. (a)	272. (c)	273. (b)
274. (a)	275. (a)	276. (b)	277. (d)	278. (d)	279. (b)
280. (a)	281. (d)	282. (b)	283. (a)	284. (a)	285. (d)
286. (b)	287. (c)	288. (d)	289. (a)	290. (b)	291. (d)
292. (a)	293. (b)	294. (c)	295. (d)	296. (a)	297. (b)
298. (b)	299. (d)	300. (a)	301. (b)	302. (d)	303. (a)
304. (d)	305. (b)	306. (a)	307. (a)	308. (a)	309. (d)
310. (a)	311. (a)	312. (c)	313. (a)	314. (d)	315. (b)
316. (d)	317. (a)	318. (b)	319. (d)	320. (c)	321. (b)

322. (a)	323. (c)	324. (c)	325. (a)	326. (b)	327. (a)
328. (b)	329. (a)	330. (a)	331. (c)	332. (b)	333. (d)
334. (d)	335. (b)	336. (a)	337. (a)	338. (d)	339. (a)
340. (a)	341. (a)	342. (a)	343. (b)	344. (a)	345. (c)
346. (a)	347. (a)	348. (d)	349. (a)	350. (a)	351. (d)
352. (a)	353. (b)	354. (a)	355. (c)	356. (b)	357. (d)
358. (a)	359. (c)	360. (b)	361. (b)	362. (a)	363. (d)
364. (a)	365. (d)	366. (b)	367. (b)	368. (a)	369. (b)
370. (a)	371. (d)	372. (d)	373. (c)	374. (d)	375. (b)
376. (b)	377. (a)	378. (b)	379. (a)	380. (a)	381. (b)

CHAPTER 7

382. (a)	383. (d)	384. (d)	385. (a)	386. (b)	387. (a)
388. (b)	389. (a)	390. (c)	391. (c)	392. (b)	393. (c)
394. (d)	395. (d)	396. (c)	397. (a)	398. (d)	399. (c)
400. (c)	401. (c)	402. (a)	403. (c)	404. (c)	405. (a)
406. (d)	407. (d)	408. (b)	409. (b)	410. (d)	411. (d)
412. (a)	413. (d)	414. (b)	415. (a)	416. (b)	417. (d)
418. (a)	419. (b)	420. (d)	421. (a)	422. (c)	423. (b)
424. (a)	425. (b)	426. (c)	427. (c)	428. (b)	429. (c)
430. (a)	431. (c)	432. (a)	433. (a)	434. (c)	435. (b)
436. (c)	437. (b)	438. (c)	439. (a)	440. (b)	441. (c)
442. (a)	443. (a)	444. (c)	445. (c)	446. (a)	447. (c)
448. (b)	449. (a)	450. (c)	451. (b)	452. (b)	453. (a)
454. (d)	455. (d)	456. (c)	457. (c)	458. (c)	459. (c)
460. (c)	461. (b)	462. (a)	463. (b)	464. (c)	465. (b)
466. (b)	467. (a)	468. (b)	469. (a)	470. (d)	471. (c)
472. (a)	473. (b)	474. (d)	475. (b)	476. (d)	477. (c)
478. (d)	479. (b)	480. (a)	481. (a)	482. (b)	483. (b)
484. (a)	485. (d)	486. (a)	487. (c)	488. (c)	489. (b)
490. (a)	491. (b)	492. (a)	493. (b)	494. (d)	495. (a)
496. (d)	497. (d)	498. (d)	499. (d)	500. (c)	501. (a)
502. (b)	503. (c)	504. (b)	505. (a)	506. (c)	507. (c)
508. (a)	509. (c)	510. (a)	511. (b)	512. (d)	513. (c)
514. (b)	515. (a)	516. (c)	517. (a)	518. (b)	519. (d)

520. (d)	521. (a)	522. (c)	523. (c)	524. (a)	**525. (c)**
526. (d)	527. (b)	528. (c)	529. (a)	530. (b)	**531. (a)**
532. (c)	533. (a)	534. (b)	535. (c)	536. (b)	**537. (a)**
538. (c)	539. (a)	540. (a)	541. (a)	542. (b)	**543. (b)**
544. (d)	545. (a)	546. (a)	547. (b)	548. (d)	549. (c)
550. (d)	551. (c)	552. (a)	553. (b)	554. (c)	**555. (b)**
556. (b)	557. (c)	558. (a)	559. (a)	560. (b)	561. (c)
562. (d)	563. (a)	564. (c)	565. (b)	566. (a)	567. (c)
568. (b)	569. (b)	570. (d)	571. (a)	572. (a)	573. (b)
574. (c)	575. (d)	576. (a)	577. (b)	578. (d)	579. (a)
580. (a)	581. (a)	582. (c)	583. (d)	584. (c)	585. (a)
586. (c)	587. (c)	588. (d)	589. (c)	590. (c)	591. (c)
592. (b)	593. (a)	594. (c)	595. (a)	596. (a)	597. (a)
598. (b)	599. (a)	600. (a)	601. (c)	602. (c)	603. (c)
604. (c)	605. (a)	606. (c)	607. (a)	608. (b)	609. (b)
610. (d)	611. (a)	612. (c)	613. (b)	614. (d)	615. (d)
616. (d)	617. (c)	618. (c)	619. (c)	620. (b)	

CHAPTER 8

621. (a)	622. (b)	623. (b)	624. (b)	625. (a)	626. (b)
627. (d)	628. (b)	629. (b)	630. (b)	631. (a)	632. (a)
633. (d)	634. (a)	635. (d)	636. (d)	637. (c)	638. (a)
639. (c)	640. (b)	641. (a)	642. (b)	643. (c)	644. (b)
645. (c)	646. (d)	647. (a)	648. (d)	649. (a)	650. (c)
651. (c)	652. (a)	653. (b)	654. (a)	655. (a)	656. (a)
657. (a)	658. (c)	759. (c)	660. (a)	661. (b)	662. (b)
663. (a)	664. (a)	665. (a)	666. (d)	667. (d)	668. (d)
669. (d)	670. e	671. (d)	672. (b)	673. (a)	674. (b)
675. (b)	676. (d)	677. (a)	678. (a)	679. (d)	680. (d)
681. (c)	682. (d)	683. (a)	684. (c)	685. (c)	686. (c)
687. (c)	688. (a)	689. (d)	690. (d)	691. (a)	692. (a)
693. (b)	694. (b)	695. (a)	696. (c)	697. (c)	698. (c)
699. (d)	700. (c)	701. (a)	702. (c)	703. (b)	704. (d)
705. (c)	706. (c)	707. (d)	708. (b)	709. (a)	710. (c)
711. (c)	712. (d)	713. (c)	714. (a)	715. (b)	716. (a)

717. (b)	718. (c)	719. (c)	720. (b)	721. (a)	722. (c)
723. (c)	724. (b)	725. (d)	726. (c)	727. (b)	728. (a)
729. (c)	730. (b)	731. (c)	732. (c)	733. (b)	

CHAPTER 9

734. (a)	735. (d)	736. (b)	737. (b)	738. (b)	739. (a)
740. (a)	741. (b)	742. (c)	743. (c)	744. (c)	745. (d)
746. (c)	747. (d)	748. (a)	749. (b)	750. (a)	751. (a)
752. (a)	753. (b)	754. (a)	755. (b)	756. (a)	757. (a)

CHAPTER 10

758. (a)	759. (b)	760. (a)	761. (b)	762. (a)	763. (a)
764. (d)	765. (a)	766. (b)	767. (a)	768. (d)	769. (b)
770. (a)	771. (b)	772. (b)	773. (c)	774. (c)	775. (a)
776. (c)					

CHAPTER 11

777. (a)	778. (a)	779. (b)	780. (c)	781. (a)	782. (d)
783. (b)	784. (d)	785. (d)	786. (a)	787. (c)	788. (c)
789. (a)	790. (a)	791. (c)	792. (d)	793. (d)	794. (d)
795. (a)	796. (d)	797. (b)	798. (a)	799. (c)	800. (c)
801. (c)	802. (c)	803. (d)	804. (a)	805. (c)	806. (a)
807. (b)	808. (d)	809. (a)	810. (c)		

CHAPTER 12

811. (a)	812. (d)	813. (b)	814. (a)	815. (a)	816. (a)
817. (d)	818. (d)	819. (c)	820. (a)	821. (c)	822. (b)
823. (d)	824. (a)	825. (d)	826. (d)	827. (d)	828. (a)
829. (a)	830. (a)	831. (b)	832. (c)	833. (a)	834. (a)
835. (a)	836. (b)	837. (a)	838. (a)	839. (b)	840. (a)
841. (c)	842. (b)	843. (c)	844. (a)	845. (b)	846. (b)
847. (b)	848. (d)				

CHAPTER 13

849. (a)	850. (b)	851. (b)	852. (b)	853. (b)	854. (d)
855. (b)	856. (c)	857. (a)	858. (a)	859. (c)	860. (d)

861. (d) 862. (b) 863. (a) 864. (d) 865. (d) 866. (d)
867. (b) 868. (a) 869. (c) 870. (a) 871. (a) 872. (c)
873. (b) 874. (b) 875. (a) 876. (b) 877. (b) 878. (d)

CHAPTER 14

879. (a) 880. (d) 881. (c) 882. (d) 883. (d) 884. (c)
885. (c) 886. (c) 887. (d) 888. (c) 889. (d) 890. (a)
891. (c) 892. (b) 893. (b) 894. (a) 895. (a) 896. (a)
897. (c) 898. (b) 899. (c) 900. (a) 901. (c) 902. (a)
903. (a) 904. (b) 905. (c) 906. (a) 907. (b) 908. (c)
909. (c) 910. (b) 911. (c) 912. (a) 913. (b) 914. (c)
915. (a) 916. (b) 917. (d) 918. (b) 919. (c) 920. (a)
921. (b) 922. (c) 923. (d) 924. (a) 925. (c) 926. (b)
927. (a) 928. (d) 929. (d) 930. (b) 931. (d) 932. (d)
933. (a) 934. (c) 935. (b) 936. (d) 937. (d) 938. (c)
939. (c) 940. (c) 941. (d) 942. (a) 943. (b) 944. (c)
945. (a) 946. (d) 947. (a) 948. (b) 949. (b) 950. (a)
951. (c) 952. (a) 953. (a) 954. (b) 955. (a) 956. (c)
957. (a) 958. (d) 959. (c) 960. (a) 961. (c) 962. (d)
963. (c) 964. (d) 965. (b) 966. (c) 967. (b) 968. (d)
969. (a) 970. (a) 971. (a) 972. (b) 973. (c) 974. (d)
975. (b) 976. (c) 977. (d) 978. (b) 979. (b) 980. (a)
981. (a) 982. (b) 983. (c) 984. (d) 985. (a) 986. (a)
987. (d) 988. (d) 989. (d) 990. (a)

CHAPTER 15

991. (d) 992. (a) 993. (b) 994. (b) 995. (c) 996. (b)
997. (a) 998. (b) 999. (b) 1000. (d)

THE RUPA BOOK OF WORLD WILDLIFE QUIZ

Replete with information on wildlifers, environmentalists, biogeography, ecosystems, sustainable development, national parks and wildlife management, this book will appeal to those concerned with helping and sustaining the essential ecological processes and life support systems on our endangered planet.

Deep Narayan Pandey joined the Indian Forest Service in 1988 following a five year stint as Forests Ranger and Assistant Conservator of Forests in Madhya Pradesh. An abiding interest in wildlife conservation drove him to visit more then 250 Indian protected areas, wildlife sanctuaries, national parks, biosphere and tiger reserves. He won the Hewetson Gold Medal for the Best Forester in 1984 and the Silver Medal for proficiency in Forest Management in 1987. He has previously written Indian Wildlife Quiz.

Also available as an **e-book**

Quiz

ISBN 978-81-716-7079-6

9 788171 670796

₹95

RUPA

www.rupapublications.com